ONE MORE YEAR

SANA KRASIKOV was born in the Ukraine and grew up in the former Soviet Republic of Georgia and in the United States. A graduate of the Iowa Writers' Workshop, she is the recipient of an O. Henry Award and a Fulbright scholarship. Her first published story appeared in *The New Yorker*, which has now printed four of her stories — a record for a writer yet to publish their first book. She lives in New York City and is at work on her debut novel.

ONE MORE

YEAR

Stories

SANA KRASIKOV

Portobello
BOOKS

Published by Portobello Books Ltd 2009

Portobello Books Ltd
Twelve Addison Avenue
Holland Park
London W11 4QR

First published in the United States by Spiegel & Grau, an imprint of
the Doubleday Publishing Group, a division of Random House, Inc.,
New York in 2008

Versions of some of these stories first appeared elsewhere: 'Companion'
and 'The Repatriates' were published in the The New Yorker; 'Maia in
Yonkers' in The Atlantic; 'The Alternate' in Zoetrope; 'Asal' in
Virginia Quarterly Review; and 'Better Half' in Epoch.

A CIP catalogue record is available from the British Library

9 8 7 6 5 4 3 2 1

ISBN 978 1 84627 177 9

www.portobellobooks.com

Text designed by Gretchen Achilles

Printed in the UK by CPI William Clowes Beccles NR34 7TL

CONTENTS

COMPANION 1

MAIA IN YONKERS 27

THE ALTERNATE 51

ASAL 73

BETTER HALF 101

DEBT 131

THE REPATRIATES 153

THERE WILL BE NO FOURTH ROME 179

Acknowledgments 231

ONE MORE YEAR

COMPANION

SINCE SHE'D ARRIVED IN AMERICA and gotten divorced, Ilona Siegal had been set up three times. The first man was not an ordinary man but a Ph.D. from Moscow, the friend who'd arranged the date said. When Ilona opened her door, she'd found the Ph.D. standing on her front steps in a pair of paper-sheer yellow jogging shorts. He was thin, in the famished way of grazing animals and endurance athletes, with folds of skin around his kneecaps and wiry rabbit muscles braiding into his inner thighs. Under his arm he held what, in a moment of brief confusion, Ilona took for a wine bottle. But when he stepped inside she saw that it was only a liter of water he'd brought along for himself. Their plan had been to take a walk around a nearby park and then go out to lunch. But the Ph.D. had already been to the park. It wasn't anything special, he said. He'd just gone jogging there. He didn't like to miss his jogs, and since he'd driven an hour and a half out of his way to meet her he'd gotten in a run first. Ilona poured him a glass of grapefruit juice and listened to him talk about his work at Bell Labs. He reclined in his chair, his knees apart, unaware that one of his testicles was inching out of the inner lining of his shorts. Ilona stared at his face, trying not to look down.

The second man was American, somebody's co-worker, brought along to a party to meet her. He had graying red hair and his light lashes were coated with dandruff-like flakes. He took Ilona to an outdoor concert at the local community college. Afterward, she waited while he searched the cabinets of his kitchen, finally producing a tray of crackers and a dry triangle of Brie. All she remembered now of the man's small apartment was the blinding light of his empty refrigerator.

The last man was too young for her and obviously gay. He'd agreed to meet Ilona because he had the impression that she was an illegal who needed to marry to stay in the country. As soon as they sat down at an outdoor table at a café, the man told her that he wouldn't normally consider such an offer but his mother had fallen ill and he needed to pay for her treatment. Ilona nodded in sympathy and asked the young man to repeat himself more slowly. She understood that her case had been shoved so far into the recesses of her acquaintanceships that the people who now gave out her phone number no longer knew who she was or what she wanted.

It had not always been this way. There had been happier times, when she'd had both a husband and a lover; when she and her husband had thrown parties in their Tbilisi apartment that went late into the night, with longer and longer rounds of toasts and the smell of sweat and sharp cologne overpowering even the odor of cigarettes. Nothing fed

Ilona's spirits more than the company of men. She loved the sound of their hoarse voices, the amateur authority with which they spoke about world affairs and other matters they had absolutely no effect on. But most of all she loved the flattering light of their attention. After the last female guest had said good night, and she had found herself in the thrilling half-susceptible state of being the only woman at the party, was when modesty came most easily to her. It lent coherence to her whole character, so that she could finally be her most humorous and disarming self. But all that had been a world ago and she tried to think about it as little as possible, now that she came home to an apartment that was not hers, and to a man who was neither a spouse nor a lover but who seemed to demand more of her than either possibly could.

"Have you met Thomaz?" Taia said. "He's outside."

"The Georgian?" Ilona went to the sink to rinse off her hands. "I hope you didn't invite him here for me." Her fingers were grainy with the watermelon she'd been slicing. She ran them under the tap and felt around on the counter for her rings.

"I didn't invite him at all. He came with the Gureviches."

"He's a bit young, no?" Ilona slipped on the bigger of the three rings first, a teardrop diamond in a five-prong setting.

"If you're comparing him with your roommate," said Taia, who almost never referred to Earl by name. "Don't lose those." She glanced down at the rings. "One day you'll take one off and it'll fall down a drain. Some women don't even wear the jewelry they own. They have copies made."

"So maybe I should tear off a piece of tinfoil and wrap that around my finger instead?"

"Do what you want," Taia said.

There was no point, Ilona decided, in reminding Taia that before Felix started making money, Taia had been so cheap she'd gutted empty tubes of Crest, scraping the toothpaste from the creases. No matter how tough her life got, Ilona thought, she'd never lower herself to something so miserly. At least she made use of the nice things she owned. Unlike Taia, whose kitchen had floor-to-ceiling pantries, brushed stainless-steel *everything*, and polished granite counters that she touched only when she was throwing a party.

"Did you put new low lights in the ceiling?" Ilona asked.

"It was Felix's idea." Taia tipped her head back. "He thought we'd get more for the house if the kitchen was brighter."

"You're selling it?"

"Not right away. It usually takes a year."

"You didn't tell me."

"We haven't really told anyone. Except the Kogans, and the Weinbergs, in case anyone knew of anyone who was looking. It isn't a secret."

There were plenty of things that Taia forgot to tell her—but selling a house? Was that just another bit of information exchanged between people with money, like a stock tip?

"Oh, don't be upset. A year's a long time. You can still come here whenever you need to get away from that man. Come this weekend. We're going to Providence for Parents' Day. You could drop in and water the plants, feed the cat." Taia laid down her paring knife and stood up. "Let me find you a key."

"I still have the key from last time," Ilona said. She couldn't tell if Taia was offering her a favor or asking for one,

just as she couldn't judge if her friends kept things to themselves to protect her feelings or because they found her irrel-
evant. She knew they gossiped. A year ago she used to bring
up Earl in conversation all the time—told her friends stories
about his two favorite activities, researching his genealogy
and organizing his video collection, and mimicked him mer-
cilessly even if he was in the next room, or precisely because
he was in the next room and didn't understand a word of
Russian. She was staying with him so she could save up for her
own apartment. But lately she'd started to realize that unless
she wanted to move north into Putnam County or south into
the Bronx, and either way end up an hour's drive from her
job, her sojourn would have to drag on for at least another
year.

She stepped outside and into the sun. The clouds were
coasting slowly in the sky, forming metallic reflections in the
second-story windows. The air was smoky from the grill. On
the patio two men were lamenting the loss of jobs to Banga-
lore. Ilona walked past the Kogans and the Ulitskys, past the
women reclining in white lounge chairs. It was mid-
September, but already she felt a kick of cold in the air. She
wore a silk blouse, while the others had come in cotton
sweaters. She set her cup on the refreshments table and bent
down to refill it with seltzer. A few dead leaves had fallen on
the grass. They were the weakest leaves, the lemon-lime color
of early fall.

When she turned around, she found Felix standing behind her. "Where is your friend today?" he said, and sur-
veyed the people scattered around the lawn.

"When I left, he was still sleeping in front of his sixty-inch
television."

"So Earl fell asleep and you snuck out?"

"Do I need Earl's permission to see my friends?"

"No. But I thought you'd extend the invitation to him."

"And what makes you think I didn't?"

"I don't think he would have missed an opportunity to be seen with you."

She was too tired to play this game today. Every time Felix tried to make her feel better he only made her feel worse. It was his diplomacy that was the worst of it, his awareness that every comment could be taken as a potential insult. The old contrite song, not for their affair of eleven years ago—which, thankfully, no one had learned about—but for all the other disappointments in her life.

"Earl couldn't come because he isn't feeling well. He's still weak from his bypass." It was a lie, an obvious one, because five months had passed since Earl's surgery. But who was going to argue? She picked up a plate. "I'm going to get something to eat."

"Please do." Felix stepped back a pace and returned her evasiveness with a delicate smile.

It was her fault for allowing Earl to meet her friends in the first place. She'd brought him along to the Fourth of July party a year ago and introduced him to everyone as her "roommate." As though this would explain anything. He was seventy, she was forty-five. She may as well have called him her chef or her architect—it would have sounded more plausible. The minute she left him alone, he'd drifted off into an empty hallway. She'd discovered him an hour later in the foyer, talking to Felix about Hiroshima. Laughter from the party floated in from the yard while Earl went on about the Japanese who had jumped into the Motoyasu River only to be scalded alive by boiling water.

She felt her heels sinking into the lawn as she walked.

Most of the other guests were wearing loafers or sneakers. A few had gathered around the grill to listen to the Georgian, the man Taia had mentioned. It was hard to tell if he was handsome or not; Ilona had seen him on the way into the party and had noted the light-gray eyes and crooked lower teeth, a combination that stirred an almost queasy sympathy in her. He looked younger than the men around him, possibly as young as thirty-five, yet he appeared to be on the brink of a decline that might be rapid, so that, when he finally did age, he would do so overnight.

"They told me they were guarding a base," the Georgian said, as the men parted to make room for Ilona. "They said that their friend had been shot in the hand and needed drugs to relieve the pain. I offered antibiotics, but they wanted morphine." She had no idea which war he was speaking of. It could have been Abkhazia or South Ossetia. She'd left Georgia three years before the republic had split from Russia, and its new problems—which autonomous province wanted independence next—had little impact on her. She'd heard of addicts in Tbilisi raiding hospitals even in peacetime. Perhaps it was the snobbery of distance: nothing would ever change there.

"I wanted to get out," he went on. "But when I stood up, one of them was pointing a rifle in my face."

"But you had a gun!" one of the men interrupted. "You should have shot him in the mouth!"

"Which mouth?" another said. "There were two of them!"

"I did something more dangerous than that," the Georgian continued. "I began to curse. I called them every name I could think of, hoping to alert someone who might overhear me. But I was running out of profanities."

He paused, glancing at Ilona. He looked surprised by the silent attention he had drawn.

"Aren't you going to tell us if you survived?" Ilona asked.

"Thank you," he said, nodding. "I did survive." He had a long jaw with a dimpled chin; it was the only feature that lent any merriment to his face. "I heard a vehicle drive into the hospital yard. The addicts thought it was a carload of soldiers. But it was only a man with an attack of pancreatitis."

"Pancreatitis? He must have been an alcoholic," Ilona said.

The Georgian acknowledged her mutely with his brows. He waited for the people around him to disperse into smaller groups. "He was. You work in an alcohol clinic?"

"No, a urologist's office. But I was a nurse in Tbilisi," she said.

"And what do you do now?"

"Catheters, rectal exams. Technically I am only a receptionist, so I also pick up the phone. But that's the only *legal* thing I do."

"Then your work is closer to medicine than mine," he said. "During the day I lay carpet."

"And at night?"

"At night I clean supermarkets."

"Then I wish you luck finding something more suited to your skills."

The man's eyes flitted across her face, as if they couldn't decide which part to examine first. "That may be hard for me to do without a work permit. My visa expires in a month."

"And after that?"

He shrugged. "We'll see. I am Thomaz," he said, offering his hand. She squeezed it lightly. "Ilona."

He held on to her fingers. "In my life I have met only two Ilonas, and both of you are very beautiful."

She felt heat rising in her face. So he is this kind of man, she thought. He was standing close, and she had to look up to speak to him. "You live in the city?" she said. Thomaz aimed his dimpled chin at a heavyset man with a short, square beard.

"Yosif is a cousin of my friend in Chiatura. He and his wife are letting me stay in their apartment in Brooklyn. Their son is at college and I'm taking his bed. It is awkward some- times. I help buy food. If I have to use the bathroom at night, I tiptoe. But I'm not complaining." He touched his hand to his heart. "I am grateful. I feel as though I need to lose three limbs and an eye before I can be sorry for myself."

An illegal who cleaned supermarkets . . . She smiled to herself. This was all they could find for her? And yet she sus- pected he knew his appeal to women, and that in the worst of times he could still rely on it.

"It is a nice place here," he continued, looking around the property. Ilona followed his gaze down to the small rec- tangular pond. A dog was barking in a distant yard. "All this space," he said, shaking his head. "I am inside all the time now. It has been too long since I've seen woods, nature. The spirit starts to forget."

"This is hardly nature," she said. "But if you want to see nature, you should come back and walk the trails. I could pick you up at the station. The trains run every hour."

Her voice had slipped into the perfect fluency of half- truth. When was the last time she had gone hiking? The sun and the mosquitoes bothered her.

"You live nearby?" he said.

"Not far."

"In a house like this?"

"An apartment." He was staring at her fingers. "I share with a roommate," she added clumsily.

"You are not married, then?"

Ilona gave a bland, cheerful laugh. "Not anymore."

"Your rings. I didn't know . . ."

She straightened her fingers and examined her hand at a distance. "Some might say they are extravagant. But I invest in living."

"Who knows here?" He laughed. "There is a ring for everything. For university, for fiancé, for boyfriend."

"Well, some of them were gifts," she said. "But not con-tractual ones."

By the time Ilona got home it was dark. The dog was at her feet as soon as she unlocked the door. "Quiet, Elsa," she whispered, and knelt down to let the dog lap at her palm. On its short dachshund legs it followed Ilona down the darkened hallway, where she slipped off her shoes and set them on a shoe rack next to Earl's. Heel to toe, their feet were practi-cally the same size. It seemed perverse that, given all the things in the world they *didn't* have in common, shoe size would be something they shared. She walked barefoot across the carpet to where Earl lay dozing on the couch. A plaid throw hugged his hard ridge of stomach. The air was stale with the yeasty scent of bread. Earl had probably spent the af-ternoon grilling cheese sandwiches, buttering the pan to get a good, deep fry. Ilona leaned over the couch and tugged a creased newspaper out from under Earl's knees, then picked up his bottle of hypertension pills from the coffee table. A glass of water had left a bloated white stain on the wood. Ilona lifted it and rubbed at the polish, but that made it worse. She carried the pills and the glass into the kitchen, which was separated from the living room only by the switch from carpet to tile. "Like mopping up a child's ass," she said to the dog, which waddled in after her.

The room she slept in had once been Earl's office. He'd cleared it out for her when she moved in, and now tall file cabinets and a gray plastic computer desk occupied one side of the living room. She'd asked him to get rid of them, but he said he needed to have all his old files available in case someone from the insurance office called. Six years the man had been retired.

Ilona rolled up her sleeves and lowered her hands into the sink. Earl was muttering something in his sleep and turning over on his side. A growth of silver stubble had sprouted on his cheeks. He barked a cough and opened his eyes. "What time is it, Luna?" he said, slowly rotating himself into a sitting position. He squinted at the clock on the VCR. "Seven-thirty? That can't be right." He found his glasses, adjusted the pads, and pressed them to his nose. He had a thick nose, German and retroussé, the kind glasses easily slid off.

"You told me you were coming home at six. Didn't we have plans tonight, Luna?"

"Did we?"

"It's Saturday, Luna. I had to call Delmonico's twice so they'd hold our table." She ignored him and continued rinsing. When had going to Delmonico's become one of her duties? Now that the maître d' greeted them as Mr. and Mrs. Brauer, Earl didn't like to miss a Saturday night. She dumped out a teacup and began to untwine the wet string from the handle.

"It's a good thing I called," he said, and raised his heavy body off the couch.

Ilona tossed the tea bag into the trash. "Call or don't call. They always say they'll hold our table, Earl. Because there's nothing to hold. Every time we go to that restaurant, it's half empty."

"You don't like Delmonico's now?"

"I don't care, Earl." She rinsed a plate and crammed it into the drying rack. "Does it matter what restaurant we go to this week? Can I just finish these dishes?"

His lower lip hung open as he searched for a thought.

"Earl."

"What?" He looked up, a white hair from his brow drooping into his eye.

"We have to trim your eyebrows."

His eyes scrolled up. He licked his thumb, then smoothed it over each brow. When he finished, he took a few silent steps toward his room. Ilona waited until he had closed the door, then wiped her hands on a hanging apron and went into her room. She could hear him moving around on the other side of the wall. She knelt down beside the old-fashioned trunk that doubled as her night table. There was barely enough room in the tiny closet for all of her things. On good days she tried to imagine that the office she lived in was a cabin on a ship and that she was in the middle of a journey across the Atlantic of another century. Kneeling, she removed the densely packed sweaters and beaded scarves one by one until she found a flesh-pink cashmere sweater. It was finely combed and as thin as lambskin; she had thought about saving it for a more interesting occasion. But now she bit through the plastic line of the tag and snapped it off. There would be other items for other occasions. She allowed her new clothes periods of latency that could last weeks or even months. This way, when she finally did take off the tags, it was with the satisfaction of unsealing a ripe bottle of brandy. And if some people thought she was extravagant, she was only preparing herself for a future that was far more uncertain than theirs. Would Earl ever have knocked on her door if she had looked any different? Would he have asked her to join him for a neighborly cup of coffee the very week she'd decided to move out of her apartment, three doors down? Would he have given her the sewing machine she'd admired? Or a fur coat two weeks later? And while she'd had to decline the fur (it smelled like naphthalene and had obviously belonged to his dead wife), she'd gotten something better. Very politely she had told him that she had no room for it now, because she was planning to move out of the neighborhood. It had become too expensive for her to live here— with her credit card debts, car payments, and the money she'd paid in advance for nursing classes she discovered she had no time to attend. She spoke undramatically, but like the best actresses, she had an instinct for timing. "But Mrs. Siegal," Earl had said, "a woman like you should never have to worry about money." And that was when he'd offered her his old office. She could stay as long as she needed to, as long as it took her to get her finances in order. That had been a year and a half ago.

She could hear Earl padding around the hallway now. She pulled off her shirt and slipped on the sweater. Her eyes looked tired in the mirror. Her hair seemed a shade closer to purple than to the burgundy she'd dyed it two weeks ago. She pulled it up from the nape of her neck and fixed it with a large lacquered pin. *Right this way, Mr. Brauer, Mrs. Brauer.* That's how the waiters would greet them at Delmonico's. Did she really look old enough to pass for his wife? Or were they playing the game, too? Well, it didn't matter to her what those people believed, whether they thought she was his wife or his girlfriend or his mistress. She was happy to cooperate with whatever public fantasy he had planned. Earl was outside the door, knocking.

"I'll be a second!" Ilona called.

What was she supposed to tell people—that even if Earl *did* want to, he had his hypertension and his arrhythmia to worry about? Not to mention his prostate surgery four years earlier. For all she knew he was impotent, and it was more of a relief to him than a disappointment if she rebuffed his attentions.

He knocked again.

"Yes!" she said, opening the door.

Earl's striped shirt was buttoned almost to his chin. He stood in the doorway wearing his slacks and slippers. In his hand was a pair of manicure scissors.

"Let's do this quickly," Ilona said.

She let him watch her while she unfolded a sheet of newspaper in the bathroom sink. "Lean over, Aristotle Onassis." Earl closed his eyes and tipped his face toward the mirror. "Here's our friend," she said, finding the errant hair and snipping it. She trimmed the rest, and then with the back of her hand brushed the clippings from his moist face onto the newspaper. When he opened his eyes again, he stood up straight. "Luna, you're my angel," he said, meeting her reflected eyes.

Delmonico's always made Ilona think of a hotel restaurant. The trellis-patterned carpet, the mirrored walls, the sense that its patrons were dining there only because they were too tired to search for something more interesting. But it was expensive, and for this reason Earl always seemed to enjoy it. She watched him hitch up his sleeves and open the leather-bound menu. He took to the business of ordering with an almost proprietary seriousness.

"You can't fool me," she said, smiling. "I know you're looking at the calf's liver."

"Nah, I wasn't, angel."

"Look at this, the steak comes with bacon. How can we keep coming here after what your doctor said?"

"I've been good, Luna."

"You've been good? Is that why the apartment smelled like grilled cheese when I came in?"

"I made those for Lawrence. He came by today with Lucinda."

"Your son dropped in?"

"They asked where you were. I said you were visiting your friends. Nothing wrong with that."

Ilona stared at him. "Is something *supposed* to be wrong with it?"

"You know, they always have their own ideas."

Ilona folded her menu and placed it to the side of her plate. "What ideas?"

"They worry, you know. After the surgery. They think I ought to get an aide, just someone to come and check on me once in a while."

It was possible he was making this up, she thought, as revenge for her not having taken him to the party.

"They think a professional can take better care of you than me?"

Earl didn't lift his head. "I told them I was fine."

"It's strange the idea didn't cross their minds when you had pneumonia and I took a week off work." She sipped her glass of water.

"I told them it was silly. I'm fine. I don't need anyone."

She could see that he regretted telling her. He'd started sweating, and she felt sorry for him. Ilona took a deep breath and slid her hand across the tablecloth to pet his. "I'll always take the best care of you," she said. They sat like that until the waiter approached. Ilona looked up at the young man and smiled. "I will have the tagliatelle pasta," she told him.

"And sir?"

"He will have fish," she answered.

Thomaz was arriving on the six-twenty. She left the clinic at five-forty and drove straight to the train station. By the time she joined the snaking line of cars at the platform, her windshield was speckled with rain. She gazed at the children twisting in the backseat of the car ahead, bouncing and looking out the windows every few minutes for the silver flash of train. Finally it came, with a high squealing of brakes, and Ilona watched the crowd disappear under the covered stairwell and spill out again onto the rain-slicked street.

When she saw Thomaz, her stomach tightened. He was standing on the sidewalk, shielding his head with his hand. He wore an orange-and-coffee Windbreaker that was too large for him. Her guess was that he'd picked it out of a charity bin. He spotted her car, and she had no choice but to lift her fingers in a weak wave before she reached over to unlock the passenger door.

He got in and laid his wet backpack on his lap, then

pressed his head against the window and looked at the sky, which had dimmed to a bruised purple.

"I'm sorry," she said, turning on the radio. "I should have checked the weather."

"Maybe it will stop in an hour," he said optimistically.

But it didn't. It continued as they drove down the parkway, the heavy drops pounding the windshield and the radio bridging the silence between them. It continued as Ilona steered the car up Taia and Felix's narrow driveway, paved now with fallen leaves.

They ran inside the house and took off their shoes and turned on the heat. Ilona told Thomaz to make himself comfortable on the leather couch, while she disappeared into the kitchen and fed the cat its supper from a tin can. When she returned to the living room, he was holding a small parcel wrapped in coarse tissue paper. "A souvenir from Tbilisi," he said, handing it to her. "It's only silver, but I thought you might like it."

It was a bracelet: stones set in twisted wire like flower petals. She molded it around her wrist and leaned in to kiss his cheek. "Thank you," she said, and went back into the kitchen to make tea. It was half past seven, and Earl was probably waiting for her. She thought of taking the walk she had promised Thomaz once the rain stopped. But it was too dark now, and already she knew that she would not be driving him back to the station tonight.

She heard the TV in the background when Earl picked up.

"What are you doing?" she said.

"I'm watching *Schindler's List*."

"Can you lower the volume?"

The background voices died down. "I got the movie because you wanted to see it."

"I'm staying at Taia's tonight. Did you eat dinner?"

"Yeah, I made some canned beans."

"I left you real food in the refrigerator."

"I looked. Couldn't find anything."

"Earl, I left you chicken. And the steamed vegetables are in the glass container."

"I ate those yesterday."

"I made them for two days."

"You didn't tell me anything about it." The TV voices got louder again.

She listened silently for a moment, until she could hear his strained breathing.

"Are you still there?" she asked.

"Where am I going?"

"Did you take your pills?"

"I took them. They never do anything."

He was just being difficult now. "What is it, Earl?"

He coughed into the phone. "I've got chest pressure."

"Is it in your chest or your upper abdomen?"

"I don't know. Just . . . general."

"It's very different."

He didn't answer.

"It could be the beans," she said. "I promised Taia, but do you want me to come home?"

"No." It was a halfhearted reply. "Maybe I'll call Lawrence."

"Lawrence? If you aren't sick . . ." She stopped herself. "I'll come home if you want," she said again.

"I'll be fine."

The teakettle whistled.

"I'll call you later," she said, hanging up. She found a dish towel and poured the boiling water into two porcelain cups on a carved metal tray that she'd taken from one of Taia's display shelves. She carried it into the living room, where Thomaz had stood up. He was running his fingers over the leaded glass of a deco lamp. "It must be nice to live in a home like this," he said.

Ilona set down the tray. "I don't envy anyone."

It was hard to tell if he was smiling or sneering. His face seemed to say, "Yes, this is also an answer, but not to the question I asked."

She had imagined she'd take great pleasure in showing off Taia's house. And she was happy that he seemed impressed, as much by the high, sloping ceiling as by the heavy art books in the built-in bookcases, and even the bird's nest retrieved from the backyard, which spoke to a kind of collecting pleasure that transcended mere attainment. She wanted him to feel the character behind these things. And yet it was not her character, and she had to repress the urge to say that she might have done the room differently, that she would have placed the furniture closer to the windows or painted the walls a brighter color, a color she could wrap herself in. Thomaz circled the couch and lowered himself into the over-stuffed armchair.

"I look around here and everything is clean, nice," he said. "People work, they do well."

She knelt on the rug by the glass table and dipped a tea bag into her cup. "Not everyone. Some people fold, they lose themselves here."

Thomaz watched her. "Like your husband?"

"Maybe if he had got an earlier start, but . . ." She shrugged.

"But?"

"To make it here, you have to want to be here."

"I see. He did not want to come to America?"

"We had a good life in Tbilisi," she said, watching a ribbon of color spread in her cup. "Good job, good apartment."

"Then why did you leave?"

"Everybody was leaving, all our friends. I didn't want to be in the last wagon on the train."

How else would she explain it? she thought. Could she say that she had followed a man who was not her husband to America? A man whose wife was her closest friend and who had become involved with her only because he was leaving the country soon and thought that she would stay behind? Or that she'd stayed with her own husband because she'd been too scared to make the long journey alone? She had been thirty-two then, and without children, not young, perhaps, but young enough for her choices to seem reversible.

"My husband was an administrator at an electronics institute," she said. "You know what that means: he knew how to tell a joke, how much to slip in someone's palm. He was a smart dog. He knew when to bark and when to lick. But none of that helped him here. He tried programming, like everyone else. But it only gave him ulcers."

Her husband's whole being had recoiled from survival the way a half-asleep person recoils from the light. She had felt responsible for a while, but then war, the upheavals of independence in Georgia, had absolved her. The friends who had stayed began to write letters full of horror stories: demonstrations stopped by troops armed with shovels and clubs, backed by tanks, spraying tear gas and chloropicrin in people's faces. Then the electronics institute had closed, bankrupt without the contracts that had come from Russia. The Russian families they knew were fleeing and settling in remote towns where the government in Moscow had given them asylum and a bit of land. Even if her husband had wanted to return, there would have been nothing to return to.

"He isn't doing badly now," she said to Thomaz. "He went to San Antonio to work at his cousin's furniture store."

Thomaz leaned over the table and picked up his teacup. "Your husband's weakness irritated you?" The question seemed aimed more at himself than at her.

She answered automatically, "No. We were not a good match from the beginning."

"When a man can't support his family . . ." He was leaning back in his chair, shaking his head. "In my town the men are all dying younger. They have heart attacks, strokes. But really it is because they've lost their purpose."

Ilona looked up at him from the floor. "Have you?"

"No, because I am here." He sipped his tea and set the cup down. "When I returned from Abkhazia, I could find no work. Then a clinic gave me a job. But no one paid us, at least not with money. And now people don't go to doctors at all."

"What do they do?"

"They die at home."

Ilona rested her palm on his fingers. "I'm sorry," he said. "All these sad stories." He parted his lips to add something more, then shut them on his thought. She took his hand. The skin of his knuckles was as smooth and tough as a walnut shell. He interlaced his fingers with hers, and before she could feel her sweat or pulse he was lifting her up, as a person would pull someone out of water, until her body was

again doing what it knew and sinking deeply into the saddle of his lap.

She allowed him to kiss first her hands and then her face. She kept her eyes closed while he kissed the line of her jaw and the curve of her neck. When his lips moved down, she pressed her face into his hair and inhaled the smell of the weather that he had brought inside with him.

Upstairs he was only a flicking shadow, the taut muscles of a back and the scratchiness of a cheek. He moved his weight over her with slow concentration, the two of them conscientious to avoid clumsiness, not testing each other, careful not to trample whatever small force they'd generated. Afterward they lay together in silence. When the air became too warm, she asked Thomaz to open a window.

"Tell me something," she said when he returned to the crumpled bed. She rolled onto her stomach and ran her fingers over the straight ridges of his forehead and nose, down to the stubbled cleft of his chin.

"You were too young to have been a doctor during Abkhazia."

"I was twenty-five. I had finished medical school. I did not consider myself young. The soldiers were younger. Nobody taught them anything. They didn't even know how to part with the dead." He tugged a sheet over his shoulder, for the room had turned cool. "One night three boys brought in a fourth. I could see as soon as they carried him in that there was nothing left to do for him. They shouted at me to rescue him. One fired a bullet into the ceiling. I forced fluid into his body so his heart would have something to beat. I kept going in front of his friends. I pumped his chest, just for show. It was worse than anything I had done to a living person." He turned away from her toward the wall. His body was still stiff a few minutes later, and she knew he hadn't fallen asleep.

"Do you have children?" she asked, finally.

Thomaz rolled onto his back and breathed in the room's chill air. "I have a son. He will be twelve next month."

"And your wife . . ."

"He and my wife are with my mother in Chiatura. My parents have a house there. I will probably also stay there when I go back."

She found the crook of his arm and curled her head into it. "It's good to have a place to go back to," she said.

They awoke at noon, to the sun leaking through the blinds. On the way back to the station, she drove him through the well-laid-out neighborhoods of Tarrytown—down the tree-lined streets, through the park, and past the tennis courts that gleamed in the sun. "Maybe next time I can see your home?" he said as she pulled up to the station. She smiled and planted a dry kiss on his lips.

In a diner across the road, she drank a cup of coffee. She considered the menu and put it aside. The coffee was strong enough to quench her hunger, and soon she would return home to cook Earl's supper. She felt as if her body had taken a long, full breath. She'd forgotten the way sex could sweep the clutter from the mind, and now she wanted to sit and inhabit this emptiness a while longer.

Elsa was yapping when Ilona opened the door. The air inside was cold, laced with the bitter scent of carbon, the smell of oil that had burned and then cooled.

"Earl?" she called into the living room. She walked into his bedroom and found the bed made. "Earl?" she called again, louder.

She'd left the heavy front door open, and now someone was knocking scratchily on it.

"Hello?" Ilona said, stepping halfway into the hall.

"Mr. Brauer?" It was the woman from next door, the one Earl sometimes spoke with and called Ms. Martha.

"Do you need something?" Ilona looked the woman up and down. She was in a sweatshirt, and her thighs bulged under black leggings.

"I just wanted to see if Mr. Brauer was back." The woman cocked her head for a better look inside.

"Back from?"

"I guess you weren't here this morning, then, when the ambulance came? It was pretty early. Woke me up." The woman rested her eyes on Ilona's sweater, her handbag and shoes.

"He isn't back," Ilona answered. "Now, please excuse me. I was picking up a few things to take to the hospital for him."

"Weren't you just calling him?" the woman asked.

"I was speaking to the dog," Ilona answered.

The receptionist at Phelps Memorial would tell her only that Earl had been taken to the cardiac ward at nine-thirty a.m. Was she an immediate relative?

"No," Ilona said. "I am his . . ." She threw a glance down the hall and saw Lawrence stepping out of the large steel elevator with his wife, Lucinda. "Just a second," she said to the girl. She slipped her rings into her palm and dropped them in her purse.

"I am his companion," she said, turning back.

"Companion," the receptionist repeated to herself and searched her monitor. Ilona stepped away from the desk and threw Lucinda a sympathetic smile that was ignored. When Lawrence looked at her, his face was reproachful, but not, thank God, pained with grief. If they still had energy left for civilized hostility, she thought, Earl was certainly all right.

"How is he?" she said, approaching.

"Fine," Lawrence said. "He's fine." He seemed disappointed not to be able to tell her something worse.

The doctors had told them that it was an anxiety attack, but with a patient who'd already had one myocardial infarction, they had to take all complaints seriously. They were still doing blood work, Lawrence said. They would finish the serial cardiograms this afternoon.

"In that case I will stay with him today," she said.

Lawrence threw a glance at Lucinda. "We don't think that's a good idea," he said. Like his father, he was not tall. His hair curled in a single wave on top of his head. "He will be staying with us at our house for a day or two."

"He likes his apartment . . ." Ilona stared at both of them, confused. "This is what he wants?"

"It doesn't matter what he wants," Lucinda said. "What matters is his health."

"We like you, Ilona," Lawrence said. "But wouldn't it be better for you to be in the company of a more . . . energetic person? My father is weak. He has his illusions. But they can damage him." He seemed to be memorizing his shoes. "You can stay at the apartment for a little while," he said.

She did not ask him how long "a little while" meant. Like anyone else, Lawrence would be gracious until the time came to be cruel. Back at the apartment she set a frying pan on the

stove and poured in some oil. Through the window she could
see the trees turning dark under the softening evening sky. At
her feet Elsa nibbled a few squares of salami. Ilona cracked
two eggs and whisked them, then poured the mixture into the
pan and watched it spread on the surface of the oil. If she
left, she would take the dog with her. Earl wouldn't challenge
her on that. Her plans struck her with the kind of certainty
that overtakes the mind after a day of hunger. She could fly
to Alaska, where the men were as plentiful as salmon. Or she
could rent a cheap basement apartment in Ossining and invite Thomaz for the weekend. She laughed at the thought of
them, in a windowless, white-painted brick basement, refusing to feel sorry for themselves because neither of them had
lost three limbs or an eye. He believed that his hardships had
galvanized him, but she knew that anyone could be fearless as
long as there was no other option. In her case, it wouldn't be
so easy. As soon as Earl walked in the door and saw her boxes
spread out on the floor, he would ask her where she thought
she was going. He'd tell her to drop it all and offer to take her
shopping, and if she resisted he'd beg her to stay. How good
giving in would feel. Tomorrow, she would begin to pack.
She tipped her omelette onto a thin dinner plate, chopped
the chives on the cutting board, and sprinkled them over the
top. A little garnish always made it taste better.

MAIA IN YONKERS

IT IS ALMOST SEVEN A.M., four in the afternoon in Tbilisi.
Maia has been up most of the night, dialing her sister, waiting for Lela to pick up the phone. Lela should have called
her, hours ago. She can think of only one reason why she
hasn't: Gogi didn't pass his interview at the embassy.

At her own interview Maia had tried to stay calm when the
consulate officer asked her about her salary. She'd told him
she was an accountant at the poultry plant in Dusheti, but
didn't mention that the plant had closed down and that she'd
been sitting without work for three years. Asked about her
family, she started almost breathlessly to spread out the photos she'd brought along: of Gogi, then nine, and of her husband, Temuri. The idea was to convince the man that you
had something to return to. And so, with all the other facts
she'd omitted, it didn't panic her to leave out that Temuri
had been dead for five months. This was September 1996.

Through Mrs. Trapolli's kitchen window, Maia can see daylight draining into the sky, bleaching it in bleary transparent streaks. Gogi's visit has been a fragile thing to arrange. He bears only a minor resemblance to the photo in his passport. The passport belongs to a boy at his new school. For $2,000 the boy's parents have agreed to let Gogi borrow it, and arranged for an uncle in Mamaroneck to send a formal invitation.

She can hear Mrs. Trapolli groaning in her bedroom, waking up. The old woman has not been sleeping well since her four-poster was replaced with an adjustable steel-frame bed. Maia microwaves the milk for Mrs. Trapolli's breakfast while the call goes through.

"Lela, it's me!"

"I was going to call you," her sister says coolly.

"He passed the interview?"

"Yes."

"Can I speak to him?"

"Just don't panic. He's at the hospital."

"Hospital?" The air goes out of her lungs.

"I didn't want to scare you," Lela says. "He smoked something. He was so happy after he passed the interview, I let him go to Dato's house. Maia, I couldn't tell him no. Another guy was there, painting the place. He gave them some garbage."

"Hash?"

"I don't know. Fertilizer. Developing fluid. Something they mix themselves." Suddenly she's screaming: "I can't control him! What do you want me to do, lock him up?"

"Did I say anything? Am I blaming you?"

Dato, the other boy, Lela tells her, passed out. That was

when Gogi dashed into the alley to flag a cab to take them to
the hospital. But when he came back to the house, he saw the
painter forcing brandy down Dato's throat.

"To make him vomit?"

"Making him *drink* it, Maia! So the police will think he got
drunk. You know they don't dig deep here."

She's surprised at how speedily Lela arrives at these expla-
nations. Or maybe it is only that she, Maia, has been gone
from Georgia too long.

"Gogi threw up in the cab. The doctors made him stay in
the hospital so they could observe him. But he's all right."

For a sickening instant she imagines Gogi, not the other
boy, passed out, a stranger shoving a bottle down his throat,
dousing her son's insides with alcohol. Dato—why doesn't she
recognize the name? Who are her son's friends?

"He doesn't tell me anything anymore," Lela begins crying. "He's always in some *mood!*"

Taking care of Gogi was not in her sister's plans. Three
years ago Lela was still working for the Finance Ministry. Now
she relies on Maia to send the monthly cash: $700, more
than enough to keep Gogi enrolled in private school, pay for
his English classes and swimming lessons, and cover Lela's
expenses. Last year he also asked for a Sony PlayStation. The
year before, a Game Boy. Sometimes she sends him things he
doesn't ask for but only talks about: a portable disk player,
baseball caps—anything somebody else might not have.

"I have to go," Lela says. "I have to stay overnight with
Gogi and sleep on the floor."

"Thank you," Maia says as Lela hangs up, even though
staying overnight is what any woman in Tbilisi would do for

a child, nothing so special it needs to be mentioned. Must every simple decency now be counted?

"We brought you a present, Nana!" Amy announces as she and Dawn dash into their grandmother's room. They're here with their mother for their twice-monthly visit. Mrs. Trapolli is in her wheelchair, tugging apart the wooden jigsaw duck Maia gives her to keep her busy while she measures out her meds. Amy takes it away and hands the old woman a gift bag.

The girls aren't fat, Maia thinks, just large in that full-scale American way, filling out the last corner of their natural dimensions. At thirteen, they're already taller than their mother, Gloria, who is herself only a darker, more annoyed version of the Mrs. Trapolli in the old photographs, from when her frame was packed with many happy pounds of flesh.

"It's foot lotion," Dawn says, shaking the contents of the bag into Mrs. Trapolli's lap. "We brought nail polish, too. Maia can give you a manicure!"

"Thank you, dear," Mrs. Trapolli warbles affectionately. "And which are you?"

"I'm Dawn, Grandma," Dawn says.

"And what about you?" she asks, turning to Amy. "What's your number, dear?"

"You mean my *name*, Grandma?"

"Yes . . . what can I call you?"

"Amy," Amy says, glancing at her sister.

Mrs. Trapolli smiles and shakes her head. "They're forgetting things again."

"Who is?" Amy asks.

"She means *herself*," Dawn clarifies.

"I thought it was right here," Mrs. Trapolli says, searching for something on either side of her wheelchair. "They must have taken it back." She sighs, then shakes her head in mock embarrassment, as if catching herself being crazy. Maia has started to notice this habit more, how the same person who forgets still realizes that she forgets. The sudden bewilderment or inexplicable bursts of anger are painful to watch, but not as painful as the quiet, confused regret that follows.

"Do you like your present?" Amy asks.

"It's wonderful!" Mrs. Trapolli's eyes are alert and intelligent again. "You are my best girls."

When she finishes giving Mrs. Trapolli her pills and apple juice, Maia realigns the bottles on the dresser. She likes to keep them in the same order: Lactulose syrup, famotidine, sotalol, Seroquel, Coumadin, and now Lexapro for Mrs. Trapolli's moods. For two weeks, just out of curiosity, Maia took a half pill of Lexapro every day, but the drug left her queasy and did absolutely nothing to lift her hopelessness. It made her feel only sadder, more indifferent, and somehow overweight.

"Maia," Gloria calls from the kitchen. "Come take a look at this . . ." Gloria doesn't lift her head when Maia walks in and takes a seat. Bills lie strewn on the mustard oilcloth, including letters from Empirical Medical Services and receipts from Grassy Sprain Pharmacy. Twice a month Gloria looks at them all.

"What is this?" she says, flashing a blue bank statement in Maia's face. "She's overdrawn her emergency balance *again*?"

"We bought her new glasses," Maia says. This is true, but the meekness of her voice makes it sound like a lie.

"That's what I gave you cash for." Gloria's physical scale, along with her constant disaffection with everything, makes

Maia feel diminished around her. Maia used to think Gloria was this way because she was a courtroom stenographer, robotically typing out the lies of criminals. But she has seen other women of similar character, at store counters and behind reception desks in medical offices, women whose patience and curiosity have been so blunted that they have become the worst sort of snob, worse even than those who choke on ambition.

"Look," Gloria says, "I put two hundred dollars in her wallet last week."

"We went to the Taj," Maia says.

Gloria lifts her face heavenward, as if asking God to witness this madness. But even Gloria knows that her mother loves restaurants, and she'd rather Maia give her what she wants than struggle with her. Otherwise the old woman might refuse to be washed or, worse, to eat. Gloria adjusts her shawl, an extravagant, embroidered piece of translucent wool. In the past few months Maia has observed Gloria dressing better, rarely without a manicure, now that she has power of attorney over her mother's accounts.

"Okay, the Taj. Anywhere else?"

Maia pretends to think, then shakes her head.

"Did you see how much my mother left for the tip?"

"Three—no, four dollars?"

"Come on, Maia, I've asked you to write this stuff down."

The last time Gloria and the girls visited, they all went to the Taj together. Following Gloria back inside to retrieve a scarf she'd left on her chair, Maia had spotted the Indian waiter lifting a pile of cash from under Mrs. Trapolli's empty plate.

"It's none of your business," the waiter told Gloria when she'd demanded the money back. "It's how much she always tips."

"Shame!" Gloria had shouted, moving her eyes rapidly from table to table to rally some voiceless consensus. But the other guests had only looked down into their plates. "Shame on you!" she'd hissed, until the waiter had slapped the money back on the table to quiet her down. Maia had been startled, but also impressed, by Gloria's proficiency at bringing disgrace to another person. She'd never had a gift for such righteousness.

After Gloria and the girls had left that day, Maia had scolded Mrs. Trapolli. "You should not give away so much. You will run out of money!" But the old woman had only looked at her with a sclerotic glint in her eyes and said, "I've got enough. I want to use it before she does."

"So you paid for the glasses with my card?" Gloria asks, looking at Maia for confirmation.

"I did." She doesn't need to tell Gloria that when the cabbie delivered them to the optometrist's, Mrs. Trapolli told her she'd left her wallet at home. She'd feigned an ache and stayed in the cab while Maia picked up the glasses. Later, Maia had asked the cabbie to wait at the curb while she ran upstairs for his fare. But he had only waved her off, speeding away as soon as she'd eased Mrs. Trapolli out of the backseat.

That afternoon she searched the whole apartment for the wallet. At last, as the sun was setting, she had collapsed in tears on the sofa. "But it's right here in my purse," Mrs. Trapolli said innocently. Only then did Maia recall the cab driver's uneasy hurry. "Did you pay him while I was in the store?" she'd demanded. But Mrs. Trapolli had turned silent again, like a scolded child. The wallet, of course, was empty; $86 for a $16 cab ride!

Even when Maia had first moved in, Mrs. Trapolli was a generous woman, offering to buy her chocolates, glass figurines in shop displays. But now all the restraints on that part of her personality seem to have been lifted. Maybe she has always wanted to live like a rich person, showering others with rewards for merely being in her presence. And how could anyone punish her for this? When the past is disappearing so quickly, what's left of a person but momentary pleasures?

At last, Gloria gathers the papers into a pile and starts to button her coat. To the girls, she yells, "Are we going to Woodbury Commons today or not?" In the hall Dawn laces up her boots, and Amy snaps the metal buttons on her jacket. "I wanted to do all my Christmas shopping online this year," Gloria begins to say, absently. "But the sizes are impossible. You're a twelve in one store and a fourteen in another. I don't know why they can't make all the sizes the same, like food labels. Doesn't that make sense?"

"It makes very much sense." The easiest part of her job is to agree with Gloria when she makes such pronouncements.

"Okay, girls, we're out."

"One more thing." Maia stops her at the elevator. "My son . . . he is coming next week. I'll call Malgorzata."

"Who?"

"The girl from my agency, to look after Mrs. Trapolli when Gogi and I go to New York. I told you a week ago."

"Fine," Gloria says, as the chrome doors slide open. "But I don't remember this. You're hard to understand sometimes, Maia."

At one in the morning, Maia awakens to a deep winter chill, sits up, and pulls a scratchy wool blanket over her comforter.

In another two hours, she knows, she'll wake up again, this time damp in her flannel gown as the radiator blasts hot air. These abrupt climate changes in her room have made her think of it as the "menopause room." Whenever she goes back to sleep, she does so with this grim anticipation, aware that her own body, at thirty-seven, is nearing its own early climax. Can such rapid aging really happen from living too long by the side of an old woman? From filling her sugar drip, lifting her up and wiping down her flesh, permitting your body to synchronize itself to the meter of her dying?

When she can't fall back asleep, she thinks about Temuri: his big, sloping shoulders, his frank, curious formality. At these moments she doesn't feel that her life with him has ended, but that it's still playing underneath her present life, like a song turned down to a low volume while people talk.

The last time they saw each other, in December of '95, she had begged him to stay in Dusheti a few more days. But he had to return to Astrakhan in time for the New Year's export rush. He'd gotten his job through a cousin who'd left Georgia after the first civil war, in '92, to start a business on the Caspian, exporting sturgeon and caviar. Back then she was still working at the poultry plant, showing up every day on rumors of promised pay; if she'd stayed home, she'd have gone crazy. By the time the plant closed down, Temuri was sending back enough money to keep them all fed.

In April came the call from Temuri's sister, Luisa. He'd been shot, along with two others, after a meeting to renegotiate protection payments. "What was there to negotiate about?" Luisa had cried hysterically. "You don't outsmart Russians anymore—they outsmart *you* by putting a bullet in your head! Did he think he would be feeding cognac to some

Moscow bureaucrats?" Maia let her go on like that for a few minutes, not asking *whats* or *whys*, thinking only that Temuri was gone.

The trouble was getting back his body. Another cycle of fighting had started in Chechnya, and no planes were flying from Astrakhan to Tbilisi. They called everyone they knew in Astrakhan and found two Russian officers willing to stuff the body in an ammunition crate and fly it with a jet load of soldiers to Grozny on their next mission—for $500. Another $200 for a driver to take the crate across the mountains to South Ossetia, where Luisa's husband would pick it up and bring it to Dusheti.

After the funeral Maia had sat with her sister and Gogi on the sofa. Two weeks had passed since Temuri had been killed, and they had no energy left for demonstrations of grief. All through the burial, the *kelekhi* supper, Gogi had watched her with an adult's appraising seriousness. Now, on the couch, she sensed in him a new kind of silence—the tormented endurance of a child waiting to speak. When he quit dangling his foot, rubbing it on the carpet, he looked up at her. "Maia," he said, calling her for the first time by her name. "You'll have to do something now."

Gogi's plane arrives late in the afternoon. At the sliding-glass doors, a few chauffeurs hold up their cardboard signs; the others wait with ready faces, the slightly suppressed excitement of people in airports. She doesn't see him at the gate or the baggage claim. Of the passengers emptying out, she spots the women—middle-aged, a few squat grandmothers—all arriving to scrub toilets and change sheets. Her first afternoon in America, she'd stood outside the terminal for three hours, then four, watching the sky darken as taxis pulled up to take people home. She'd guarded the luggage while Sophiko, the woman she'd flown with, disappeared to the pay phones to dial the Brooklyn agency that had paid for their tickets. In Tbilisi they'd been told someone would meet them at the airport, but they had not been smart enough to ask for the agency's New York address. In the weak, graying sky Maia saw the blinking lights of aircraft in liftoff. In her throat she could feel a spasm of rising tears, but her bathroom trips on the plane had left her too dehydrated to cry.

At seven-thirty the woman arrived, the one who was to have picked them up at three. She did not help them carry their luggage to her van, and she said little besides "Sorry, I forgot." They drove through the low blocks of Queens into Brooklyn. From the back of their jolting van, Maia could see the shapes of smokestacks, the black skeletons of iron girders. She spent her first night with five other women in a tiny apartment whose floor was coated with a waxy film of aging dirt. In the night she'd crept to the bathroom and squatted carefully over the seat, taking care not to step in the thin brown rivulet spilling out on the tiles.

The agency had taken their passports, which were to be returned when they'd worked off the money for the airfare. In the morning they crammed into the same van, which this time took them to Rockland County. She and Sophiko were dropped off at a split-level residence that appeared to be between owners. They spent the day up on chairs, washing ceilings, until Maia felt a chip of paint drop into her eye with a hot astringent sting. "You put too much bleach in the water!" Sophiko had cried, dragging her to the bathroom and forcing her face under the rushing cold water. The last thing Maia had seen clearly were three delicate steps rising into a

half-sunken Jacuzzi. On the dark ride back to Brooklyn they
sat in the back, whispering with the tactical calm of hostages.
"We have to stop doing this," Sophiko had said. "We have to
stop, or we'll die." They left three weeks later, when Sophiko
learned of an agency that could arrange for them to look after old people. They got their passports back but were not
paid.

At once she sees him, off from the crowd, rolling his suitcase toward her. He slows down, his eyes tunneling in on her.
He is thicker in the chest and taller, but his neck is still a
boy's neck, thin. He's wearing the items she's sent him: Hil-
figer jeans and lumberjack boots, a gray fleece pullover. She's
forgotten how healthy Gogi has always looked, with his shiny
black hair that almost radiates blue, his pale skin, the pink
solar flares in his lower cheeks. His brows have turned thick
and dark, like Temuri's, nothing like the feathery watercolor
lines she remembers.

"You are here!" she says, stepping forward. She wants to
sling her arms around him but isn't sure which part to hug,
the shoulders or the waist. He doesn't make a move, only
stares back with his clumsy half-smile, his lips locked in
place, not willing to spread a centimeter farther.

"I was afraid they'd stop you at the last minute."

"Retards," he says. He tugs the passport out of his pocket.
"They're too busy checking if the photo is glued on straight
to see if it's *you*."

It's a miracle he's slipped in under so many eyes. And
maybe he was able to only because all of it is a game for
him. He's still a big child, with a child's magical oblivion to
danger. This is why children win Olympic medals, she
thinks, why audiences go to hear ten-year-old violinists;

at their age, the music is still more real for them than the crowd.

On the train back to Yonkers, Gogi is quiet, watching the river of homebound traffic. He glances around at the commuters, men with briefcases on their laps leafing through the *New York Post*. He turns back to the two-toned world outside the window, and his eyes follow the cars on the expressway that narrows with the tracks, then angles away sharply into the engulfing wilderness. He finds little to see out there besides the beige cubes of storage depots, walls defaced with graffiti, a row of retired school buses bafflingly painted white. These are the back doors of towns, their ugliest parts, Maia thinks. She is ashamed that this is what Gogi must see first.

The elevator greets them with a faint odor of cat piss, a scent she's breathed in so many times she can smell it now only because Gogi is inhaling it, too. The light is on in the living room. Malgorzata sits on the couch with her eyes closed, a magazine wrinkled in her lap. She twitches awake. Maia opens her wallet. "Everything was okay today?"

"She wanted to go outside," Malgorzata says. "So I rolled her to the elevator. She told me, 'I prefer to take the stairs.' "

"She forgets she's in the wheelchair sometimes."

"I said no stairs. She made so much noise, I took her back inside."

She pays Malgorzata while Gogi walks in ahead, stepping onto the deep carpeting. He touches everything, the brushed-aluminum lamps, the paneled drawers. When Maia closes the door and turns around, he's staring up at the oil painting, a desert sunset lit like a masterpiece under its own spot-lamp. He looks at her and sniffs the air. The apartment

doesn't reek like the elevator, but the smell is stale and me-
dicinal, only weakly masked by the dry cinnamon potpourri.
In their phone conversations she left all this out. Here it is,
she wants to say. Here is where your mother wakes up in the
mornings and goes to bed at night.

"Who's this?" He picks up a photo of Dawn and Amy.

"Her granddaughters."

"They're fat," he says, and puts it down again.

Maia heats up lamb *kharcho* for him on the stove. The refrigerator is stuffed with food—chicken in walnut sauce, pie
with salted cheese, and red bean soup. He doesn't want any of
it tonight, he says. They were fed on the plane. "Do you sleep
in the same room with her?" he asks.

"I have my own room, Gogi." She is stunned by the question—hasn't she complained a dozen times about the venge-
ful radiator in her room? On the phone last week he
reminded her of a pair of headphones she'd promised to
send him and forgot. But this fact about her life he can't remember?

While he goes to wash up and change into pajamas, she
puts freshly laundered sheets on the couch. A new tooth-
brush is next to the bathroom sink. When he comes out, he
crawls under the blanket and props a pillow behind his
shoulders. She sits down on the edge of the couch. "I'm going to read a little," he says, as if in warning.

"That's fine. I'll just sit here." She smiles. He takes his
book off the lamp stand. On its jacket is a picture of deep
space with a single levitating planet that looks like Earth except for the unfamiliar pattern of continents.

"I'll see you in the morning, Maia," he says impatiently.
She stands and kisses the top of his head while he finds his

page. In bed, she listens to the shallow sounds of Gogi coughing and shifting, until the band of light at last goes out under her door.

In New York City nothing impresses him. He drags his feet when they run to catch buses. "Why do they have their flag hanging everywhere?" he asks every five blocks. "Is it a holiday again?" For two days this goes on.

On the third morning, after waiting in line at the Empire State Building, Gogi seemed to expect the elevator to ride them all the way up the building's hypodermic spire. When it let them out at the observation deck, on the eighty-sixth floor, he turned disappointed and moody and wandered away from her. She'd stood there, facing the Whitestone Bridge and covering her ears against the stinging wind. She had given him her hat because he'd left his own at the apartment.

Afterward, crossing the runways of Park Avenue as the lights were changing, she'd grabbed his hand and hurried to beat the oncoming traffic. But in the middle of the lane, he'd let his palm go limp in hers. From the safety of the sidewalk, she'd turned to see Gogi idling behind, indifferent to the cars screeching to brake around him. And now, returning on the ferry from Liberty Island, he doesn't even look at the skyline, only at the water monotonously lapping the side of the boat.

They've filed in behind a crowd of fourteen-year-olds, a class trip. The boys busy themselves spitting over the side of the boat. Some of the girls compare souvenirs. They wear no hats, only bright fuzzy hoods around their shoulders.

"One picture?" Maia asks, lifting her camera.

"No!" Gogi snaps, glancing sideways at the teenagers.

"Please, Gogi, before the view disappears." All day he's refused to be photographed. She has four empty rolls of film in her bag. "You're embarrassed in front of *them*? You'll never see them again."

"Why do you push, Maia?"

One of the girls, pointing her camera into the foggy distance, says, "She's got a small head."

"Fool, how many pictures you need?" says her friend. "It's a statue. You act like she's got a hundred of them expressions."

"Don't stare, Gogi."

"Why do they talk like that?" he asks.

"Like what?"

"Like they don't know English. They live in this country, don't they?"

She's speechless. Who taught him this? Where does this antipathy come from? "They understand each other," she says. "What's wrong with you today?"

Gogi cranes his neck and gives her an impassive look. The rest of him stays slouched over the metal deckside. What is so grotesque about her kindness that he needs to punish her for it? To Mrs. Trapolli, he's courteous and sweet. In the mornings, he asks the old woman if she slept well, if she wants anything special to eat. Last night he carried her warm cereal to her, and she told him she was proud of him, as if to account for the possibility that they might be related.

"Don't you like this trip?" Maia asks.

Gogi shrugs. "I can see it on a postcard." He turns back to face the water.

"Look at me!"

"What?" he asks too loudly. The girls glance over.

"You don't want to do *anything*. What do you want to do? Go back and smoke your insect poison with your friends—go!"

Gogi narrows his eyes and takes a step back, as if she's a crazy person on the street. "Then don't show it to me!" he shouts suddenly. "Why are you showing me all of this? I can't stay here anyway!"

More people on the ferry turn to look, but only for a second. This is New York, after all, where the only faux pas is to express surprise.

"Gogi," she says quietly. "What do you want to see?"

He opens his mouth, starts to say something, but stops himself.

"Anything you want," Maia says. "We'll do it."

"Beauty and the Beast."

"The musical, for children? You want to see that?"

"Yes! What's wrong with it?"

She recalls the signs up in Times Square, the advertisements on buses all over town. Of all the things they've seen, this is the one that got stuck like a bramble in Gogi's imagination.

"Okay, we'll go," she says. Such a sentimental thing, really, for a boy his age to want. But maybe not. Maybe, away from his friends, such a desire isn't so strange at all.

At the two o'clock matinee she's amazed to see not just families inside but also adults, elderly women paired off or sitting by themselves. The auditorium is domed and ornate, sealing off the noises of the street.

"Do you want a drink from the lobby?" Gogi asks, leaning over.

"A drink?" She opens her bag and passes him the small

juice box she packed before they left the apartment this morning. Gogi examines it like a curiosity, then hands it back to her.

"Maia, I didn't say *I* wanted a drink," he whispers. "Do *you*?"

She can't help herself. All her tedious selflessness—no wonder he finds her tiresome. She can smell her shampoo in his hair, bends forward and kisses his head as the lights start to dim. He doesn't jerk away this time. He doesn't smile either, but for a second something like a shadow of pleasure seems to pass over his face.

Fairy tales, even here, Maia thinks, when the play begins. A few weeks ago Sophiko told her about an Armenian woman who worked on Central Park West, looking after a lady whose son was a Wall Street tycoon. Every Saturday she chaperoned the old woman to her brunches in West Hampton, the same restaurant for three years. Now, everyone learns, she's become engaged to the chef. Meanwhile the tycoon, who's on the board of trustees at a college upstate, arranges for the Armenian woman's seventeen-year-old son to come study on scholarship. True story, says Sophiko.

Maia has met her for lunch in Manhattan while Mrs. Trapolli is at one of her full-service checkups. "Is she beautiful?" Maia asks. Sophiko shrugs, as if to say, Who *knows* what their type is here? Sophiko works as a nanny now, looking after children with long names like Jeremiah and Adelaide.

"I'll tell you what the problem is with these Americans," Sophiko loves saying. "Their mothers telling them all the time they are *so* special. Then they grow up, and nobody is good enough for anybody else."

Back in the day-lit lobby, Gogi's skin glows with rest.

"Should we take the subway back to the train station?" she asks.

"No. Let's walk," he says. "I want to walk." The lamps are on, up and down along the street. In the last hour before twilight, the light seems to be taking a rest and settling evenly over everything.

She can still return to Dusheti, she thinks—not be alone anymore. But who would pay for it all? Or she can commit to staying here—hire someone to marry her, pay rent on an empty apartment so she can show a joint lease to the immigration authorities, get her green card. All of this takes money, and coordination, of which she has little at the moment. Gogi is leaving the day after tomorrow. This is all she can think about right now.

"Tell me," she says. "You and Dato smoking that junk, it was only one time?"

He keeps walking, looking at the window displays, the hood ornaments on the parked cars.

"Dato smoked too much," he says. "He's one of those people who gets stupid two hours a day."

"Who gave you that stuff?"

Gogi shrugs.

"Listen to me. Those people don't care what happens to you—they only want your money."

"He didn't ask for money."

"Then they'll ask for something else. You don't want friends like that."

"It can have some advantages." His grin makes him look idiotic, she thinks, like one of the hoodlums idling on Rustaveli Avenue, leaning up against the buildings all day as if their backs were holding up the walls.

"Remember when Lela got robbed?" he asks. "If you know

one of them, you can pay a commission, and they return everything. But if you're their friend . . ." He smiles. "If you're their friend, you don't get robbed in the first place."

"If you were friends with them, Gogi, they'd make *you* do the robbing for them. You understand?"

"God, Maia," he says, rolling his eyes. "Why do you talk to me as if I'm a half-wit? I'm not saying I *like* them."

"Good. They have nothing to like."

He turns back to the window displays. For almost a whole block, they've been walking past a sporting goods store. Gogi's eyes move from snowboards to a red canoe dangling by chains from the ceiling.

"Do you want to go inside?" Maia asks, leaning on the glass door and pushing it open. She wants him to see all this, to imagine some world other than the one he knows—a world where people live more vital, graceful lives, where they go sledding and skiing and paddling boats.

"Maia, look!" he says, walking past the snowshoes to a re-volving rack of puffy jackets. They hang in every color, but he pulls a black one off the rack and holds it close to his chest. "It's getting cold at home. This won't take up any space in my suitcase. I can wear it on the plane." She can see him getting fixated, getting ready to act wounded if she says no. He slides his arms into the sleeves. "What do you think?"

She finds the tag on the zipper and pulls it closer: $300. "You don't need it," she says. "You have the one I sent you."

"This?" he pinches the fleece underneath. "Maia, I need something *serious*."

"Then buy one in Tbilisi. It'll be cheaper."

"It's all Turkish-import crap. They don't even have the logo." He runs his hands along the shiny black quilting and turns to examine himself in the mirror. "You had money to send Lela a leather coat."

"Don't act deprived, Gogi. I sent Lela a coat because her coat was stolen when she was robbed."

"And what if *my* coat is stolen? *Then* you'll send me this? That makes no sense, Maia. We're already here."

"You plan on getting your coat stolen?"

"No, that isn't what I'm saying! You're here. I'm here. What's the point of my even *coming*? Sitting on a plane for twelve hours just to—" He stops, aware of his misstep.

"What's the point of your *coming*?"

He looks down and inhales sharply through his nose.

"Take it off right now," she says. She should slap him. She should leave her handprint on his spoiled face. A handprint, he might understand. "Now!"

They don't speak on the train, or in the elevator. In the apartment, a draft from Mrs. Trapolli's room carries in the familiar smells. Once Malgorzata is gone, Maia turns to Gogi and points to the couch. "Make your own bed tonight."

He unlatches his backpack and flings it onto the couch. "Did I ask you to make my bed?"

"No. You don't ask for ordinary things."

"I don't need your rags, Maia! You're here. You can keep your crap here."

"You know why I'm here!"

"I *don't* know anymore. Every year you say 'It's one more year, one more year'!"

She opens her mouth to speak, but can't. His words are like knocking blows to her heart.

"Maia!" Mrs. Trapolli yells from the bedroom.

Mrs. Trapolli is deep in her chair when Maia runs in, a cross-hatching of tiny veins reddening her cheeks. "There's someone in the house," she whispers hoarsely.

"No, Mrs. Trapolli, it was only me and Gogi."

"Somebody was shouting."

"I'm sorry we scared you."

"Where is Gogi?" Mrs. Trapolli says.

"Gogi!" Maia shouts into the hall. "Come say good night."

He drags himself in and stands in the doorway. "Good night," he says, and circles around to leave.

"You're being rude, Gogi."

"What's wrong?" Mrs. Trapolli raises her face to Maia. "Is he angry at me?"

"No, at me. I didn't buy him a jacket."

His eyes narrow with anger. "Why are you telling her?"

"This is true, Gogi? You want a jacket?"

"No!" He looks at Maia. "I don't want it. And it's too much money."

"It's not *about* money, Gogi!"

But Mrs. Trapolli is no longer listening to them. She's leaning over her armrest and taking her pocketbook out of her dresser.

"No, Mrs. Trapolli," Maia starts, as Mrs. Trapolli reaches in with a shaky hand and plucks out a tight roll of cash.

"Come," she says, nodding at Gogi and holding up the pile with a trembling wrist.

"We can't take it, Mrs. Trapolli," Maia begins.

"You're talking nonsense!" she snaps. "It's my gift—*my* gift!" Her eyes glow like a fanatic's. This isn't about politeness; it's a point of honor for her.

"Come over here," Mrs. Trapolli commands.

"Go," Maia says softly. "Take it."

She can put the money back in Mrs. Trapolli's purse to-morrow. But what about Gogi, making him take it, then tak-ing it away again—how long can she keep doing this to him?

Mrs. Trapolli grabs his hand, stuffs the cash in his palm, and closes his fingers over it. "I want to see the jacket tomor-row."

They stand, saying nothing, until the radiator stops hiss-ing, and the room becomes quieter than even their silence.

At the airport terminal, she thinks: Always, fewer going than coming. Some of the passengers for Gogi's flight are college students. Also a few portly businessmen clutching laptop cases while they check in their bags. Gogi's suitcase is bulging, bloated like a bug with all the things he's bringing back, gifts for Lela and the family, indulgences.

"Let me take a picture of you," she says, when he gets his tags. He poses against the terminal's glass doors, tucking his thumbs into the pockets of his new jacket. It does something for him, she has to admit. They had taken the bus to the mall in the morning and found the one he wanted. What can you really teach your child, she thinks, by denying him? At home, they paraded it in front of Mrs. Trapolli, who clapped her hands while Gogi took it off and put it on again.

"You look expensive in it," Maia says. He tries to resist smiling, but the supressed smile is even more pleased-looking than an ordinary one. In front of the security check, she snaps another photo. "One more," she says, shyly.

"Promise you won't work so hard, deda," he says when he hugs her good-bye.

He takes out his ticket to show the airport attendants.

And here she is, going through it again—the separation she
never thought she could bring herself to make the first time.
From behind the security check, he waves to her one last
time, then rolls his bag down the corridor. He's flying east,
with a stopover in Frankfurt. Tomorrow he'll be back in
Tbilisi, walking up Sololaki's cobbled streets, past balconies
throwing their diagonal shadows over the lime-washed walls.
The whole view will be steeped in a dying yellow sun. His pillows and sheets will be in the living room where he left them.
She won't take them off or fold up the sofa for a few more
days. She'll sleep there at night, while the radiators spit and
hiss down the hall.

THE ALTERNATE

SOME OF THE WEDDING GUESTS had started filtering out the
doors. Victor looked around for Vera and saw her in the
lobby, pointing to her watch. She didn't want to stay late, she
had told him. She needed to be fresh for her doctor's appointment in the morning.

"I'll tell Alina your boy will call," Anna Davidovna said
when she kissed him good-bye and Victor patted his wallet to
reassure her. Victor had asked for the girl's number on behalf of his older son, though he had no intention of passing
it on to Stas. That would be wasteful, possibly even reckless.
He'd written down her number on the back of a dollar bill,
having picked up the idea from a man at work, one of the
young traders who liked to brag about keeping his girlfriends'
telephone numbers recorded on pieces of cash in his wallet
to avert the suspicions of his wife. Victor usually felt nause-
ated by such vain disclosures, but the idea had appealed to

him, even though he himself had never had a use for it: with a dollar bill, a man could easily feign ignorance. And when the affair was over, he could go and buy himself a cup of coffee.

The maroon carpet in the lobby was matted down with footprints. Women dashed around, handing their purses to their husbands to hold while they hunted for coats. A small crowd had gathered around a bulletin board montage of the bride's and groom's childhood photos. Alec, the father of the bride, whom Victor had met sixteen years earlier in Vienna, when their two families had lived in the same hosting facility, stood in the middle explaining to his friends that the wedding had been carried out in Orthodox tradition on account of the groom's family. The groom himself was only *Modern* Orthodox, Alec explained. It was an important distinction.

"Modern, not Modern, what's the difference?" asked a man wearing a shearling.

"If it's forbidden but you really want to, then it's okay!" said Alec.

"Back when we lived in Queens," Vera interrupted, "we knew one Modern Orthodox couple." She glanced over at Victor, then carried on. "They had a little girl and two boys. Sometimes the boys wore their *kipas* and sometimes they didn't. Maybe they thought God performed spot inspections."

All were silent for a moment, then Alec and the man in the shearling broke out laughing. "Spot inspections, that's good," Alec said, clapping Victor on the shoulder as if he had made the jab. Except that Victor hadn't found it so funny.

"Wait until it's our turn for a spot inspection," he said morbidly.

His wife stared at him in bewilderment, a small crease of spite forming between her thin brows. He knew what that look meant: when exactly had *he* become such a Big Jew?

And all he'd done was start reading those Telushkin books before bed.

If he wanted to find spirituality, she'd told him one night, why not spend an evening at the Met? That was *different*, Victor had tried to explain to her. But she never really listened. She said she found *all* religion a little depressing and primitive, even after he'd explained to her how it was all wrong when people said "an eye for an eye" was savage. Wasn't it better than having your whole head chopped off for an eye? That's what the Jews had given the world! Temperance. *Only* an eye for an eye! That was Civilization. It was all there in the Telushkin books, if she was interested. It was good stuff.

Vera walked ahead to the glass doors. Victor followed her into the parking lot. She didn't want to talk about it. "I'm tired of you embarrassing me in front of people, Vitya!" she said, slapping the door.

They drove home in silence. Oh, she liked to *say* it was all religion she didn't care for, but of course she meant only his. And all these years she'd kept *her* tiny silver cross—a gift from her beloved grandmother—stored in that little zip-up pocket in her handbag. And when he had brought *that* fact to her attention, she'd howled that in thirty years of marriage she'd worn it only once, when Dr. Nathan had discovered a mystery lump in her right breast. And when subsequent tests revealed only an innocuous cyst, the cross had gone quietly back into the purse. Because it wasn't like she'd been raised by a band of pagans either. But that was what you did for the person you loved. You became a practical secularist. You became a political centrist of the soul.

A stream of headlights rushed past them, cars merging into the traffic from JFK Airport. Vera stretched her arm for the radio dial and scrolled through the channels. She chose one and leaned back. They were catching the end of a traffic report, followed by a piano interlude, a melody elaborating into a longer improvisation. In the ghostly green lights of the dashboard, Victor could see the line of stitching on Vera's sleeve. A year ago the fabric in that spot had been singed by a wayward ash from one of his cigarettes. She'd been unable to return the dress to Neiman Marcus as she'd planned, had worn it twice since, and on both occasions reminded Victor that his little ash had cost them four hundred dollars. He'd told her he preferred to consider it a gift. She finally had one decent thing hanging in her closet.

"I wrote them a check for three hundred dollars," Vera said, turning down the volume. "I think that was enough." She always thought it was enough. It was her policy never to write the amount until after she'd arrived at a celebration and taken a look around.

"You could have made it four hundred. The food alone was two hundred dollars a person."

"Who told you that, Alec?"

Victor didn't bother to reply.

"That's what he spent the evening doing? Giving everyone the itemized breakdown, just in case we were getting jealous by the wrong amount."

"It wasn't enough," Victor said.

"It was. Let me sleep." She tilted back her chair and shut her eyes.

It was no secret that Alec was "dirty wealthy" now. That was how Vera liked to say it: it was her special variation on filthy rich, the idiom she'd originally aimed for and missed. At the start of the tech boom he'd started a company that specialized in tax software, an idea that turned out to be miraculously recession-proof in the ever-changing weather patterns of the American economy.

He turned up the volume on the radio. It was Rachmaninoff's second piano concerto again, classic FM favorite, long melodies and rhapsodic flights. That was why Mila had liked playing him so much. She had tried to teach him to hear with her ear. "It's *sound*," she'd said once, "it's *supposed* to shift. It's supposed to slip away." Back in Zhitomir, where they'd attended the same music school, Mila had become fanatical about Rachmaninoff and played him at every recital. Sitting through all those trilling harmonies had made Victor want to shoot himself. But the teachers loved it. He'd even overheard one of them telling the school's director, "That girl knows what she's doing, while the rest of them are still making estimated guesses." The rest of them? Didn't that include him? But it was only after that comment that he had started to notice the swanlike rise of Mila's shoulders, her foot's cautious tilt on the pedal, the way the piano used all the parts of her and required her like nothing else did. Loving Mila had been, at least at first, so much easier than hating her. And sometimes he still wondered if love could really start that way, as nothing more than temporary relief from envy.

Victor felt around for his wallet. Still in his pocket. He'd call the girl up in the morning. Tomorrow was Martin Luther King Day; she'd probably have no classes. He would introduce himself as an old friend of her mother and ask her out to lunch. Simple as that. And if she didn't say yes right away, he could say he was calling to give her back some old photographs. Maybe he'd even bring them along. For years his pictures of Mila had been wrapped up in plastic baggies under the photo albums, excluded from the official parade of memories that gave every family its happy past.

How much had her grandmother told her? Certainly in all these years Anna Davidovna might have mentioned something to her about his and Mila's once-upon-a-time plan to marry. They'd talked about it his first summer home from college; he'd done poorly in his math classes and grown dispirited by St. Petersburg's persistent wetness. But when he'd returned to school in September, from Zhitomir, his eyes had rapidly adjusted back to the tranquil paleness, that endless array of canals and marble buildings. By the end of his second year it seemed impossible that he would have to go back again to the Ukraine after graduation, get assigned to an apartment with a low ceiling in a district thrown up from reinforced concrete. Everything was better in Peter: the streets, the jobs, the gentiles.

In October of his third year he met Vera. They were married in March. She'd grown up right on Vasilievsky Island; marrying a native of the city was all it took to get the coveted *propiska*, a stamp in his passport that let him stay in St. Petersburg forever. That was what marrying up had meant in a classless society. And what would he have gotten if he'd stayed with Mila? At best, Viborg for his first vocational posting. More likely some remote industrial hole, a run-down concrete suburb. He stopped going home for the summers after that. He did not want to run the risk of seeing her. What would he say to her with the glow of possibilities no longer ahead of them? And now running into her mother here, at a wedding! But then so many of them ended up on this side of the Atlantic eventually. An entire world transposed, like an ink blot on a folded map, from one continent onto another. The old woman had been so happy to see him. She'd squeezed his hand and kissed his face. Death, it seemed, was the great forgiver. He had been twenty-eight when his mother had called him from Zhitomir to tell him that Mila had died in a car crash, returning from a concert. From his living room window he had looked across the water to the south bank of the Neva, where a line of stone palaces appeared to float. Then he had gone into the bathroom, and with his knees pressed into his eyes, he'd wept. His tears seemed to last forever, an endless supply of salt and grief and water. But there was some other substance in that mixture, too. Some lighter element, a trace amount that altered the pH of sorrow. And what could it be if not, just possibly, relief?

Their exit was a smooth turn off the ramp from Route 684. Vera lay asleep, her arm stretched limply across her breasts. Victor drove past the steepled village library, with its glass addition, down a row of wooden porches and raked gravel paths. It was only after he and Vera had moved here, to Westchester, that he'd seen how the other half really lived on their vast estates hidden at the bottoms of gravelly driveways and concealed behind acres of overfertilized grass. He'd left his job at Systech to work with Rick, a hardware guy who had started custom-designing home security systems for the rich. So deeply secreted were those palaces, you'd think their inhabitants were Italian nobles taking refuge from The Plague. The owners were never home when Victor installed wires in their kitchens, but he saw their spacious countertops and their fancy bottles of olive oil and knew he hated them.

He pulled into his driveway slowly. The lights were off in the house. Victor turned down the radio and found the bill in his wallet. He opened it and folded it up again, then again, until almost nothing remained of it but four soft corners.

In the morning breakfast was waiting on the counter. Garick sat on a barstool lifting a spoon from his cottage cheese and watching it dribble into the bowl. "It doesn't even have to be a big pool," he was telling Vera, who stood bent over the dishwasher, unloading plates. She wore her narrow black pants and a cream blazer. Her hair was delicately combed back from her face, as it had been the night before.

"Another party?" said Victor, sitting down.

"I already told you. I have my appointment today." She left her coffee cup in the sink and picked up her bag. A faint powdery odor drifted behind her as she walked to the door. Had she put on perfume? On his behalf she wouldn't tweeze two hairs from her chin, but for her gynecologist she became Gina Lollobrigida.

Now that his mother was gone, Garick turned to Victor. "It's not like the backyard is even real grass. You guys *pretend* it's grass, but it's just dead moss."

He pointed out the window at the spotty row of trees marking their property. For two weeks Garick had been pleading for a pool. He'd become fanatical with the idea. A pool for the vital purpose of throwing pool parties! Nothing short could secure him a proper notch in the eighth-grade caste system. And the older one wasn't much better: after Stas had boarded the bus back to Rutgers, Victor had opened his Visa statement to discover a bill for $260 charged to a Westin uptown. It was dated January 1. "Three hundred dollars for a hotel room! You told me you were at a party in Queens. Who did you meet there, a duchess?"

"I'll wire you a check tomorrow! I said I will!" Stas had yelled back into the phone from the safe distance of his dorm room. "It's two hundred and sixty dollars, and you're acting like you're in Chapter-fucking-Eleven!" He could never win with his sons. Especially when the shouting matches degenerated into English, as the boys always made sure they did.

"Why don't we dig it ourselves?" Garick said, trying the enthusiastic note.

"The shovel is in the garage," said Victor. "Be my guest."

The clock on the stove read eleven-thirty, but a drab, prolonged dawn still hung in the sky. He left Garick in the kitchen, unfolded the dollar, and dialed from the family room. Three long drones, then a lifted receiver. There was no hello.

"This is Alina?" Victor said cautiously.

"Speaking." In the background someone was talking. "*I asked for one thing . . .*" For a moment it sounded like Garick. Victor could feel his stomach rocketing.

"Can you hold a minute?" said the girl, and then to whoever was in the room with her, "*I'm on the phone now. You said, put it someplace safe, that's exactly what I did.*"

"Sorry," she said, returning to the phone.

"My name is Victor. I was speaking with your grandmother yesterday—"

"Uh-oh." The girl managed a pained laugh. "She's resorted to handing out my phone number, okay. Gotta love that."

"Yes, and all of us have nice sons too," he said with a laugh of his own, to which she didn't remark. Her voice was perfectly American, like a voice in a commercial for tourism or health care, which made it inappropriate now to switch languages.

"But I am calling about something different," he continued more solemnly. "Your mother was a good friend of mine, a long time ago. Now I have learned you and your grandmother are in New York! It would be a great shame if we did not meet. I would have a great pleasure to take you somewhere you like, maybe for a dinner?" He thought about making his invitation more appealing by mentioning the photos, but decided it was best not to overstrain.

"It's nice of you," she said with appropriate sympathy. "But I really didn't *know* her."

"I understand. You are busy."

"No no, I just meant that—" She sighed, reluctant about being rude. "People try to talk to me about her, and I have nothing to say."

"I am making you uncomfortable."

"Not at all."

"I am not an unpleasant person, I promise," he said. "For an hour I can be very entertaining."

"Right. It's just that I have classes."

"On Friday?"

"No, I guess not," she said, the resistance in her voice worn down.

He found a pen and wrote the address she gave him, on Seventieth Street on the East Side, near where she lived. He repeated it back to her twice. "That's right, fine," she said. "Terrific."

And then she hung up, just as he was saying "Terrific" back, happily. Though he wondered, a moment later, if he'd botched the word. In his mouth it had sounded like "Chrifeeg!" But it didn't matter now, fortunately. He'd done it! It was like being a tournament swimmer, a chess champ at your peak moment, knowing everything you'd performed on instinct had been correct.

It was a feeling he'd held on to until Friday, a mild euphoria activated by nothing but his fingers twisting the raddled, soft-cornered, folded bill in his pocket. It was dark by the time he approached the corner of Seventieth and Third, where a brick-and-limestone condominium ascended to a few night-shining clouds. On the other side of the crosswalk a girl stood rocking gently on her heels to stay warm, her nylon jacket reflecting some of the diffuse light of signaling traffic. Her hands were in her pockets as she swayed, looking side to side, thinking or not thinking of him as the taxis cruised along the street.

In the restaurant Victor could see that Alina resembled her mother; she had the same tense pout and large, myopic-looking eyes—a more Semitic variant of that actress Rossellini. It seemed miraculous that she could be sitting across the table, lifting a fork to her lips, inhaling and exhaling.

He sat up and straightened his shoulders. "I wanted to bring a few photographs of your mother, but I forgot. Perhaps next time?" He didn't know why he was saying this, except that he'd felt suddenly the urge to bring up a next time, before it was too late.

"You don't have to do that. We have photos hanging all over Babushka's apartment." She broke more pieces of tilapia with the side of her fork. "My grandmother turned them all into little shrines, with candles and plastic flowers. You'd think we were Catholic."

"You still live with her?"

"No, I moved when I started medical school. It was too hard to keep commuting from Brooklyn. You know, for years I thought I had arthritis," she said, "but it turned out I was just living around a lot of old people."

"But when you're a doctor," said Victor, smiling back, "you'll be with sick old people all day."

"I'll be an ophthalmologist. I'll work with the ailing healthy." She lifted her full wineglass, and Victor quickly lifted his in a mock toast.

He could guess from just looking at her that a girl like Alina didn't faze out at the computer screen and bang her fist down on the keyboard like his sons, until the shift key flew off and got lost behind the furniture. No, girls like Alina probably got up and poured themselves a glass of water. If things weren't going well, they went for a jog. They edited all the errors out of their résumés instead of staring stupidly at the "Skills" paragraph after they'd already sent the thing off, wondering if they really had meant "Excellent Good Oral and Communication Skills."

"The other students, they think as practically as you?"

"I don't know how they think." She shrugged. "But they're all amazing." One already had a degree from divinity school, she said, and was going on to become a hospital chaplain. Another was publishing a paper in a public health journal on the role of lesbian caretakers in the AIDS crisis. "They're very effective people. I'm ordinary in comparison."

"But you aren't ordinary at all," said Victor. She didn't interrupt him. "You made it here all by yourself, with no parents."

"I have a father," she said. "He helped how he could. He had his own difficulties here."

"Once a year, he sends her a gift card to that underwear store," Anna Davidovna had told Victor at the wedding. The man had immigrated to Minneapolis after Mila had died, and the grandmother had been raising the child ever since.

Alina took a tiny sip of her wine. She'd worn a woven sweater that showed her hollow collarbones. Victor could imagine her easily at thirty-two, or forty. Her narrow build would make her look younger than she was.

"My grandmother never thought much of him," she said. "I guess she wanted to see my mother with you, right?"

She'd probably heard the story and more than once, he decided, conceivably a kinder version. "She told you that?" he said.

"In her way. She and her friends are obsessed with 'keeping' a good man. That's how they all talk, like the Second World War just happened. Half the men are dead, and you'd better be grateful for the amputees. That's the kind of math they're used to."

"You are hard on them."

"I'm not. Have you ever listened to them? You'd think all of Minsk and Odessa were populated by professors. Every teacher was the director of a school, and all the nurses were doctors."

Had the grandmother really been singing this tune for years? he wondered. That their split had been Mila's fault?

"Every morning," Alina went on, "it was like I had to get up and travel to America again on the subway. I'd be walking along to the F train stop and all the geriatrics would already be outside on the benches, comparing their grandkids' starting salaries or whatever it was they did that early."

She was trying to be funny, but there was some shade too resolute in her voice. She had lost too much time living with these old cottars.

Victor leaned in toward her. "You have to think of them like children. They are dreaming of what they'll be one day. Except they dream it backward instead of forward."

"Like children," she repeated. And for the second time he caught it, the lopsided smile of the original.

It was seven o'clock and people were trekking in and out through the heavy restaurant doors. A raw moist draft had slipped in under the circulating air. Alina lifted her sweater up over her neck and slipped it off. For a second her skin emitted a warm blast of something at once floral and caffeinated.

"I lived around the corner from this restaurant for months," she said, glancing around at the orange tiles on the walls. "But I didn't even know about it until my boyfriend's mom took us here. She was giving a speech at a banquet for runners, the night before the New York Marathon. Everyone was eating giant bowls of spaghetti."

"Your grandmother didn't mention a boyfriend."

"I'm sure she didn't."

He backtracked. "His mother, she also runs in the marathon?"

"Both of them do. She and Joel run every year. Very effective people, I told you."

Effective. The word made him think of home appliances. Where did she learn such unlikely words? No one he knew talked this way, especially not his children.

"She gives speeches on the psychology of endurance," Alina said. "Actually she's considered an expert on it. Ten years ago her charter plane crashed in Alaska. She survived two weeks on moss and lichens. The search and rescue made national news, then she wrote a book about it. Ever since, she's been getting invited to give motivational speeches to athletes."

"This is really very super." He didn't know what else to say about it. He thought of the woman eating snow out of her palm, chewing on a twig. The psychology of endurance, did such a field really exist? Had this woman named it into existence? It seemed ludicrous in a way possible only in this country: spinning your own survival instincts into a new form of expertise, peddling them as though they were something you could teach people.

The girl touched her fingers to the cold pane of the window. The two-toned world outside was fully dark now. She withdrew her hand and examined the moisture print on the glass. It wasn't that he'd done poorly for himself, Victor thought. But the truth of it was, others had done better. It had been Alec's success with the tax software that had emboldened him to team up with Rick. But the company was filed in Rick's name only, and two years into their venture Rick had dropped Victor for two Czechs with overstayed visas—each willing to work for half of what Victor took. Since then he'd retrained as a computer network specialist and now he spent his afternoons monitoring firewalls, dragging himself from office to office to identify malfunctions caused by people fat-fingering their passwords. It was well compensated but tedious work. The networking specialist, he'd come to realize, was the sanitation ant of the computer world, suffering the endless connection and reconnection of cables, keeping the forest clean. But who knew? When the economy picked up he might start doing the work on a contracting basis, turn himself into the great frontiersman known as the Independent Consultant, a businessman of sorts.

He watched Alina scrape the last morsel of fish and scoop it into her mouth. With her face lowered she looked more like Mila. But when she lifted her chin again, he saw that her looks were set in a totally different key, with heavier eyelids and an Irish scatter of freckles covering even her lips.

"When I called the other day," he said, looking straight at her, "you sounded like you were fighting with somebody."

She stared up at him in surprise, still chewing. "You heard that?"

"I heard only a man's voice."

Her hand had disappeared under the table, but now she brought it back up to touch her head. She appeared uncertain about how much she wanted to say. "Joel, my boyfriend, came over to tell me it was my fault he almost melted his laptop." She stopped and glanced over her shoulder, as if suspecting someone might be listening. "In the morning I was locking up his apartment. The landlord changed the locks and the new key didn't fit. I paged Joel at work. He told me I could leave the door unlocked as long as I hid his laptop. But nowhere *obvious*, like under the bed or in the laundry basket. He lives in a building with a doorman and security cameras, and he's terrified of getting robbed."

An aproned waiter reached in between them to take their plates. Alina leaned back to let him. "So I put it in the oven," she continued. "And then I left. When he got home he set the oven on preheat because, who knows, he wanted to bake himself a potato."

She sat up straight again and exhaled. "I don't know how that was *my* fault."

"No," Victor said. "Of course not. But you told him where you put his laptop, yes? You left a message?"

"I thought I did." Alina shrugged. "But maybe I didn't."

If only he could make sense of this girl, her strange mix of agitation and liveliness. She seemed overstimulated, like she'd been running on nervous energy all day. Maybe now she was looking for a reaction from him, trying to see herself cast back through another person's judgments.

"Did you do this on purpose?" said Victor.

"I didn't think he would actually turn on the oven. But the possibility crossed my mind, so maybe I invited it."

What kind of answer was this? It was a way of thinking he couldn't master. In the universe she inhabited, it didn't matter *what* you did as long as you were able to formulate a response to it afterward. It seemed to him an American trait. People never tried to determine if their actions were harmful or indecent or cowardly. What they needed to know, instead, was whether they were intentional or unintentional, candid or insincere.

"I guess the dybbuk is always inside us, just itching to get out," she said.

"Last year when I still smoked," Victor said, "I burned the sleeve of my wife's dress. It was at somebody's birthday, in one of those restaurants with dancers and mirrors. She made a joke at me, in front of people." All he remembered now, he said, was holding his Marlboro above her sleeve's sequin embroidery, black sparkling on black. He'd tapped his cigarette gently and watched the ash float down like a dead leaf, glowing red at its edge. "I don't know if I did it on purpose or not, but I remember I was very happy."

Alina's eyes became wide, appalled and impressed by his deviance.

"It doesn't mean you're a bad person," she said.

"No. We are both good people," said Victor.

He felt ready to talk, if she would listen, about the unsolvable decisions of his own youth. He wanted to tell her how he had lurched into adulthood—into married life with someone he'd known a few months, and with an impulsiveness only children were capable of. Though it would probably overwhelm her to hear all this, would force on her a too stark perception of him. What he wanted now, most of all, was for her to like him.

After dinner they walked without hurry back to her building, past the mahogany bars and chained bicycles. Garbage bags sat piled against the parking meters, green fluorescents from a margarita bar reflecting off their black plastic skins. The wind had picked up, swaying a Lotto sign in front of them. Traffic was rushing down East Seventieth Street. Victor rested a custodial hand on the back of Alina's Nordic jacket. They stopped on the curb and watched the traffic light that would turn at any moment.

"It isn't like I don't have these grand aspirations," she said. She had a little wine on her breath, which he could smell in the nearly icy air. "It'd be nice to go to the Amazon and join Doctors Without Borders, for example. But mine is a different situation." The light changed to green, and she turned to him with an exhausted look, as if to say that her case was much too complicated for an immediate explanation. "Last night Joel told me he listed Boston as his first choice for a residency. There are plenty of good programs in New York, but he wants to be at the *best* one, of course. And I'm in last place again."

She stumbled at the lip of the sidewalk, and Victor caught her arm gently, though she pretended not to notice and only drew her big hood around her head, stepping into the street.

"He told me I should do my internship there when I graduate. But he *knows* I can't leave my grandmother. She doesn't have anyone else in New York, and the city subsidizes her housing."

"But it's only a few years, yes?" Victor said. It was a mystery to him how these internships worked, but he wanted to offer her something. "You can still have, how do they say it, 'a long-distance relationship'?"

"Maybe," she said, raising her brows. "But that didn't work out so well for you, if you don't mind me saying."

"Well, this was not the same thing," he corrected her. "You live in a free country. Our laws were idiotic. It would not have helped if your mother came to Leningrad. Neither of us would have been able to stay there. You had to marry someone in the city to stay." This sudden self-disclosure surprised him. They'd approached a lit passageway between an underground parking garage and what he guessed to be the lobby of her building.

She searched his face. "So what are you telling me, that you chose Leningrad?"

"It was more complicated."

"Well, and now you're all here anyway," she said.

He felt an urge to explain, to tell her she didn't have it completely right; he hadn't been one of those so desperate to stay in St. Petersburg that he was willing to settle for some shapeless, yapping girl.

But she had an absent expression again, her big fatigued-looking eyes already somewhere else. Her shoulders rose up lightly, in a way that showed she was anxious to get out of the cold, which had made his own gloveless fingers feel nearly frostbitten inside his pockets.

"Here's my building," she said.

Through the panel glass doors of the entrance Victor could see a red leather couch in the atrium and a deserted security desk behind it. It was obvious she wasn't planning to invite him into the lobby. In the lit and busy restaurant where they'd sat, she had relaxed her vigilance over some wine. But now, on the icy street with garages and dry cleaners around them, she wasn't much drawn to whatever yearning was keeping him standing there, longer than necessary.

"I'm glad we could meet," he said.

"Thank you for the dinner."

He nodded. There were spots of color on her cheeks from the cold. He wanted to reach across to touch her arm, though this would be unwise; she had no wish to deal too directly with whatever connection he perceived between them. She lifted her mittened hand in farewell and went inside, and he watched her run to catch the elevator that was just then opening.

He wasn't sure what to do now. Finding his car and driving the long hour home was a defeat he wanted to forestall. The alternative, to look for a bar and sit alone among the loud and crisp-shirted yuppies—the sort he configured networks for every day—made him queasy. He knew it had been irrational to expect much from the meeting, or to think that his time with her would yield some lasting meaning. You didn't necessarily know what motivated you until afterward— he remembered this, suddenly, from their conversation. It had been irrational to think that she might have something in common with him, or to be drawn to him, or forgive him by some cosmic proxy.

The wind had settled. He looked at his watch; it was nine o'clock but seemed later. He started his trek back to Seventy-second Street, where he had parked. On the opposite side of the street a discarded Christmas tree lay on its rubber platform inside a fenced playground. More black garbage bags sat piled up on the curb, where store owners had also left bundles of serrated cardboard boxes tied together with white yarn. He thought about Vienna, his first Western city, after St. Petersburg. His and Alec's families had meandered its labyrinth of fountains and picturesque streets for days on end. It had been an almost supernatural feeling, to be pedestrians finally under the free skies of Western Europe. And then one afternoon Alec had returned to their *pensione* from the post office carrying a cardboard box. When he had knifed it open, Victor saw that it was filled with only tea and chocolates. But as Alec peeled back the silver wrapping of the candies, he showed the others what was tucked inside: hundred-ruble notes, to be exchanged for shillings the next morning. Alec had addressed the box to himself in Vienna two weeks before his departure. No one had been allowed to leave with anything but a few suitcases and exactly $123, American. But there were no laws against sending yourself packages abroad. It was such an obvious solution, it only seemed illegal. For years Victor had thought that his own fate in America might have been sealed in that initial failure of resourcefulness.

A few meters away Victor could see a man sitting on the concrete stoop of a locked beauty salon. He was spreading his knees and drawing them in again, as if performing thigh exercises. His ski jacket was missing its zipper, and by his feet lay a natty wool cap. He had the distinctive appearance of the city's well-looked-after homeless. *"Excuse me, sir,"* the man said, all the loose skin on his bony face smiling imploringly. Victor searched in his pocket before the beggar launched his pitch. He felt no desire to be hustled tonight. The bill was still there, creased in half against the pocket lining. Victor withdrew it, fixing momentarily on his own elongated ballpoint scrawl—Alina's phone number printed over the ONE and the pyramid's surveying eye. He bent down and dropped the dollar in the cap and was rewarded with a "God bless you." This was the trick, he thought walking ahead, to do it on the first impulse, before any wiser notion could overtake you.

ASAL

THE OTHER WOMAN CAME to Gulia's apartment late in the morning, after Rashid had left for his trip to Munich. He'd flown out of Tashkent while the sun was rising, to transact business with a resort developer who wanted to buy his rugs. At four the two of them had woken up to sip coffee, waiting for the driver to arrive. She had fallen asleep again for a few hours, on Rashid's side of the bed, until it was time to get Layli ready for school.

Around eleven the doorbell rang, two short chirps followed by a looping canary twitter of someone holding down the buzzer. When Gulia opened the door, she knew who it was—*the nun*, clasping the cuff of her long sleeve and staring up at her the way a child would stare at an elephant. The woman's face glistened in the October heat, the top of her forehead covered by a *hijab* of gray chiffon draped tightly under her chin. She glimpsed past Gulia into the darkness of the apartment.

"Who are you looking for?"

The woman ignored her.

"You forgot your manners?"

"And *you*?" the woman said. "You plan to keep me standing here all day?" She stepped inside and led herself through
into the living room, eyeing the wool rugs on the floor from
Rashid's factory, before glancing at the twin bouquets of roses
on the table, which Rashid had brought home a day earlier for
Gulia's thirty-first birthday.

"I'm Nasrin," she said, inspecting the collection of Bo-
hemian glass on display in Gulia's wall unit.

"I know who you are."

"You bought all this yourself?"

"What do you need to know that for?"

"He doesn't buy me such things."

Her face was long, heavy in the jaw, her eyebrows virtually
triangles, Gulia noted, untouched by tweezers. Only once, at
a large wedding in town, had she seen Nasrin up close. Gulia had come with Rashid, while Nasrin had arrived on the
arm of Rashid's mother. In the carnival atmosphere of a
wedding it had been easy for the two of them to keep a mea-
sured distance from each other's tables.

Nasrin was relaxing into one of the dining room chairs
when Gulia returned with tea from the kitchen. She had un-
wrapped her *hijab* and was fanning herself now with her hand,
as though she were beside a kiln. Her hair was black, like Gulia's before she'd started dyeing it copper. But coarse strands
of gray already appeared in the thick part, and above her
temple, a coin-sized patch was almost completely bald, like
the skin of an animal who'd clawed out its own fur.

"Mother-in-law told me you were ugly, but I see you are
not bad looking," Nasrin said.

Gulia reached over to pour herself tea. Whatever village they'd plucked her from, she thought, Rashid's family had obviously forgotten to teach Nasrin how not to fart out gems like this.

"I won't lie, you are pretty," she added. "You are five years older than me, but you look young."

She had the same little-girl voice Gulia knew from the phone—a voice that had once called her a divorced prostitute and declared her womb a barren pit. It wasn't unusual for Nasrin to force both of her howling children to wail into the phone before hanging up. Gulia had come to expect these calls whenever Rashid went out of town on business.

Gulia set the teapot down between them. "What do you want here?"

"I came to say I cannot live like this anymore. You think I don't see how my husband treats me? Like I'm a puddle he has to step over every day."

"What does this have to do with me? I was here before you came around."

"No one told me about you. Is it my fault everyone deceives me?"

You could tell from the woman's face, Gulia decided, that it cost her nothing to open her mouth and lie. Just as it cost her nothing to shriek into the phone and leave clumps of cat fur and needles on Gulia's doorstep. Nasrin would never admit to such witchcraft now, passing herself off as a good Muslim, taking up the *hijab* to please Rashid's mother, who with her own deranged ideas had all but turned the family into a clan of Wahhabi fanatics. The doorstep gifts had seemed like a joke at first, the hexes of a backward villager. But the fact that in their nine years together Rashid had succeeded in making Gulia pregnant only once, and that even *this* had ended with miscarriage, made her worry that the cat hair and broken eggs, the oaths and curses, had thrown something off balance in her.

"No one told you about me?" Gulia said. "Half of Fergana knew, and *you* didn't?"

"I thought we could get along. My uncle has two wives in one house, and they live like close girlfriends."

"I'm not interested in your family or how you were raised."

"And how were you raised?" The woman started up off her chair. "To become a divorced prostitute and keep a man away from his children!"

Again, the children. Nasrin had announced her first pregnancy just weeks after Rashid and Gulia's own wedding party, when they'd gone to a mullah and then invited their friends to a restaurant—everyone from Gulia's job at the bank and their circle from the university attending to support Gulia, the real wife. Afterward Rashid had begged Gulia's forgiveness, explaining that Nasrin's pregnancy was the result of the wedding night, when proof of a soiled sheet had been unavoidable. He swore he had not slept with Nasrin since then and didn't plan to again. And for almost a year he had kept his promise, spending his nights at Gulia's apartment, their life together interrupted occasionally by the five o'clock morning phone calls from Rashid's mother, reminding him to be home for his first *namaz* prayer. But after a year of neglect, Nasrin had started to complain to the relatives. "People will talk about me," Rashid told Gulia. "It's a sin not to sleep with your own wife." Could she not wait a little longer until he divorced Nasrin? Hadn't he, after all, waited for her the same way?

When Nasrin's second child was born, there were no more

apologies. "What are you so sad about?" Rashid had asked in-
differently. "You already have a child. If it's not enough, have
another!" There was nothing to say back. Was she going to
deny him the right to have his own children?

But now she wanted the woman out of her apartment.

"In all this time if he had left me," Gulia said, "I would
have made peace with it. It's not my fault he loves me. But
you have known all along that he stays with you because of his
mother."

"And is it because of his mother that he sleeps in my bed
when he's not here?"

Gulia smiled. "Leave these stories for your friends."

"You don't have to believe me now. You will soon
enough."

Nasrin placed her hand on the arch of her back as she
stood up, stomach first. She was ready to go now that she had
delivered her news, and began to wrap the chiffon around
her face again, taking final stock of the room as she tucked in
the last strands of hair. It was almost noon. The megaphone-
aided voice of the muezzin was booming though the window,
enduring for blocks, while Gulia, from her chair, her palms
attached with sweat to the warm porcelain of her cup, watched
Nasrin walk herself to the door, wobbling slightly as though
carrying a precious weight.

Gulia pushed the swing every time the chains rocked her way.
The breeze was lifting flyaway ends of Yoni's hair. His legs
dangled from the black rubber harness. In a sandbox a few
meters away, a small boy was picking up his toy cars and talking to each one in inflections that were unmistakably an
adult's lecturing to a child. It seemed the rule at the play-

ground beside Sloan-Kettering on York Avenue that the smaller children—offspring of doctors from the hospital housing—were all white or Indian, while the older kids filling the basketball court after school were either Spanish-speaking or black. A boy in shorts down to his ankles jogged the ball sloppily to the free-throw line, the cement absorbing every slap and echoing it back across the warm stupor of the late afternoon. Gulia watched a skinny old woman in a sari approach the child who had been talking to his cars and pull his arm, making him holler. In her five months in New York, Gulia had never spoken with any of the other nannies or grandmothers who sat around the playground benches. All of them seemed to be living out private, mysterious patterns of their own. Only the big, lacquer-nailed women from the Islands chirped among themselves in West Indian accents while their kids sat dumbly in their strollers. The few Russian nannies she'd encountered didn't suspect that she could comprehend them. On the streets of their own cities, they might guess correctly that she was a Tajik, but here on East Sixty-eighth Street, where she was camouflaged among so many unknown races, she was one more undifferentiated face of the East. The Russians were fat and blond, wearing eye shadow the colors of street chalk, as though they'd only just discovered that they could still wear makeup after fifty, and their lives as women did not yet have to be over.

Now that she had become invisible, her past had also started to slip away, to another orbit, almost beyond her reach. When Rashid had returned home from his business trip, she'd told him that she didn't intend to wait for another child of his to be born. Even in his tortured state, he'd laughed at her and gone on pretending she wasn't going anywhere. Even when she'd found the Jew lawyer in Queens

who'd sent over the bridegroom, Rashid had refused to believe she would pursue her plan to the end. But there was no
public record of their marriage, she reminded him. They
had been married by a mullah, without ever going to the civil
registry—something it had been too late to do by the time her
divorce cleared. By then, Rashid's mother had already found
Nasrin.

Gulia had arranged to meet the American bridegroom at
the Club Hotel 777 on Pushkin Street. She had paid both for
the hotel and for the interpreter, to show the man around and
so she wouldn't be seen with him alone. Sitting under the
awning by the swimming pool, Gulia had looked into the
stranger's gaunt face and seen, for the first time, her own pain
reflected in the huge pity of someone's eyes. She understood
enough English to figure out that the man was a loser, a
drinker and a gambler. But he was human and ashamed of taking so much money from a woman for his meager services. In
a gesture possessing whatever impoverished honor he had left,
he'd handed the interpreter a hundred-dollar bill and asked
him to buy Gulia a gift from the hotel shop. "The lady isn't in
need," the interpreter had said, and told the man to put away
his money. Before the American flew back to New York, they'd
gone to one of the wedding registries and signed all the papers.

One of Yoni's sandals had dropped to the ground again. Gulia bent down and dusted it off while he wiggled in his harness, red-faced and grunting. She hoisted him out and
sniffed at his diaper, getting a whiff of the sweet lacteal reek,
then kneeled to strap him into his stroller and pried his
moist fingers out of her hair. He was on the whole an easy
child, smiling at her with his duck lip. A feeling of attach-

ment had grown between the two of them in the very first week, when she'd wheeled him around the East Side, still worried that people were looking at her and seeing a servant, noticing the incongruity between her dark-eyed, high-cheeked face and the ginger-haired boy who was clearly not hers. But no one noticed them. Nobody in this city cared about her at all.

On the sidewalk, chips of mica sparkled where the sun hit them. It was the beginning of June, and the freshness of spring still hadn't become tarnished by the heat. Gulia pushed the stroller along toward the apartment blocks of First Avenue. At the bottom of her purse, her phone was chiming through its fragment of the *Carmen* overture. No need to guess who it was.

"Allo . . ."

"Asal . . . ?" He didn't ask for Gulia anymore, only for his Asal—his honey, his darling thing. "I called you this morning. You didn't want to talk to me?"

"I was bathing the boy, Rashid."

"And yesterday night?"

"I went out for groceries."

"Asal, don't lie to me. Who goes out at ten at night to buy vegetables? I know people in New York."

Was it possible, she wondered, for him to carry on a conversation without hinting that she was being watched by spies?

"I picked Layli up from school yesterday," he said in a hopeful voice.

"She can walk home. It's only ten minutes to Auntie's house."

Her mother's sister was now looking after Layli, the way

she'd taken Gulia herself in at fifteen, when her mother had died and her father remarried.

"Your aunt should keep a better eye on her," Rashid said. "I drove past the school, and she was hanging around in front with the boys. I told her, if any of my friends or workers saw you right now, they would laugh at your father."

"Always thinking of yourself, Rashid."

He didn't answer her, and she could tell by the long, hurt silence that she'd been uncharitable. Rashid had always treated Layli like his own, even better.

"You think I don't worry about you?" Rashid said. "They make you go out at night, by yourself!"

"Ten o'clock at night is no different from four o'clock in the afternoon in Manhattan."

"Right," he said. "Manhattan of the rich. Tell me, are there Negroes in Manhattan?"

She sighed. "Yes, there are, Rashid."

"If a rich Negro starts chatting with you, will you go out with him?"

"Why are you asking me these silly questions?"

"Would you marry a Negro, a very rich one?"

How about a Jew? she wanted to ask him. How would he feel about indiscreet, soft-waisted, slightly cheap Vlad, who'd asked her to lunch twice before she'd relented? Would Rashid give her one of his unconvinced, patronizing smiles, or would he see that even the attentions of someone as unlikely as Vlad could restore something back to her, not hopefulness exactly, but at least an awareness of herself as someone who could be loved?

"Stop teasing me," she said. "You know I can't marry anyone while I have my 'husband' in Queens."

"Ah. The card shark. Has he gambled away your money yet?"

She paused the stroller in front of the Cigar Inn and let Yoni gape at the polished wooden Indian outside. "It's his money now," she said.

Yoni jacked his neck back, fastening his eyes on the Indian's angry painted face. It was his favorite part of the afternoon walk, this unmerciful colossus that had the power to captivate some primal part of his toddler brain.

"Asal, how long do you plan on torturing me with this nonsense?" Rashid said.

"Until you decide we can live like normal people, the way you promised me."

"You want to know how I live *now*? I work all day. Then I go and sit in some restaurant until they shut the doors, so I don't have to go home to her."

"We've been through this old song . . ." She pivoted the stroller in the direction of the Sotheby's building. "I need to change the baby."

"All right, I'll let you go, *governess*. Tell me, Gulia, do you still love me?"

"It's the middle of the night for you," she said. "Go sleep."

The Governess. He always made up new names for her when he called. Fräulein, Mary Poppins. She'd managed to avoid telling him about all her other chores: the cooking and laundry, the swishing of chlorine around in the garbage pail, the donning of grim rubber gloves, as she was doing now, to scrub the toilet. In the big room Polina's breast pump hummed with its motorized drone. Gulia skinned the last paper towel off the cardboard roll and wiped the porcelain rim of the toilet, then peeled off the gloves again to fetch another roll from the kitchen.

Polina was on the couch, her blouse undone. Two clear suction cups milked her breasts with a hungry mechanical force while she read the newspaper on the coffee table and scooped lentils out of a bowl in her lap. Gulia had expected her to be out of the apartment by ten, but Polina had decided at the last minute to send her husband out for diapers before their drive to her mother's. "Vlad called for you," she said without looking up. "You were in the laundry room. He wanted to make sure you're still meeting at one."

Gulia's stomach stiffened. "He asked me a long time ago. I didn't want to be rude to him." It embarrassed her that she and Polina had to speak of it.

Polina lifted her underslept, anemic face and examined Gulia with a grin so subtle it eluded explanation. "By all *means*. If you aren't interested, it's your business."

When she had invited Vlad a month ago for a Shabbat dinner, Polina's aim had been to set him up with a woman from her hospital, a fellow resident. There had been a lot of exaggerated smiling over red wine, talk about travel and TV shows Gulia didn't watch, even while Vlad listened to the woman's stories about her dog and without much diplomacy aimed amused surreal glances in Gulia's direction.

"If I'd known he was your type," Polina said, going back to her paper. This was the kind of statement she was adroit at making: one that could mean nothing or everything. Possibly she was reminding Gulia of their conversation two weeks before, when Gulia had talked about her Bukharan Jewish friends from school and then had gone on to say she could never marry one—and it would be the same if she married a

Shiite—that her lineage would be cursed for seven generations. But all she had really meant was that she was so cursed
already, she didn't want to call down more trouble on herself.
It seemed impossible to clarify this now, especially with
Polina's pager suddenly beeping from somewhere deep in the
creases of the couch.

"What's with these people!" Polina moaned, switching to English. She stuck her fingers between the cushions, her milk
dripping down the vacuum tubes that had stretched her nip-
ples to the size of small fingers. A minute later Gulia could
hear her from the bathroom, ordering one of the nurses to
pull a patient's chart.

Gulia squeezed a few hard sprays of Windex on the mirror and streaked off the foam. As abrupt and hard-to-read as
Polina could be, the fact that she had neither the time nor
the inclination to monitor every move Gulia made had
turned out to be the saving grace of Gulia's job, the one thing
that didn't make her feel like a servant. In her first husband's
house, she'd spent entire afternoons scrubbing and sweeping
like Cinderella with Morad's mother shadowing her from
room to room, finding fault with everything. It ached her
now to remember how her student years had flown past,
never going out to a café with her friends, every evening
keeping her mother-in-law company while the old woman sat
up watching television late into the night. And then having
Morad lunge at her in the mornings with his schizoid suspicions, tugging off whatever pretty shirt she'd picked out for
class and forcing her into some dowdy grandmother blouse.
It was just as well, to cover the brown bruises on her arms. All
of this Gulia had kept from her aunt, feeling the crushing
blame of her own decision. She'd married Morad in spite of
her aunt's reassurance that there was always enough room in

her home for Gulia, that there was no rush to be married off. Her aunt had demurred to the women who'd started paying visits when Gulia turned seventeen, telling them that the girl was still too young. Though none of this discouraged the mothers, all looking for a daughter from a good family, a *good* girl. The pressure to leave her aunt's house, Gulia realized now, had been mostly in her head, though there had also been the rush of being desired, if not by the boys directly, then by their mothers. Picking a husband the year she'd turned eighteen had been like picking pastries in a shop. The one she had liked was a light-eyed, worshipful medical student who was an Arab, but on this matter her aunt had firmly set down her foot. As a consolation, she'd consented to Morad, the best looking of the others, in spite of the heroin rumors already floating around. They'd had their wedding the summer before Gulia entered university.

Two years later Rashid was the only one who noticed how many times a week she missed lectures. After class she'd find him on the student-swarmed steps between the lobby and first floor, holding his neat notes for her to copy. His face was still rounded out by a moon of fat in those days. It would be another year before he'd tell her to leave Morad. "My family is all I have," she'd informed him. "I can't make an orphan of my daughter."

"Then do it while she's still young," he'd reassured her. "She'll know me as her father." He was gifted like that, when it came to making promises.

Looking into the pond, Gulia could see the reflections of the terraced buildings along the park's eastern border. Their shapes were distorted in the surface of the water, where a

duck was pushing itself along, cutting through the crisscrossing eddies made by the wind. Gulia touched her hair to make
sure it hadn't fallen out of place.

"You put it up, didn't you?" Vlad said, casting a sly off-
center look at her from under his cap, which had a little umbrella and the word citigroup embroidered on it. "I like it. You
should wear it up more often."

She smiled faintly, unsure of what to say to such a compli-
ment. Rashid would never remark on how she had assembled
herself. He'd leave the tricks of technique alone and regard
her only as a radiant whole.

"So you want to know why Polina hired you?" Vlad fished
out a box of mints and shook a couple into his palm. He
beckoned Gulia to take one. "She said she showed all the
other potentials the kosher kitchen, and you were the only
one who got nervous about mixing up the dishes. She said
anyone that stressed out by it was probably honest."

He chuckled and looked at her admiringly. He seemed to
relish this naïve idea of her as an obedient domestic.

"Why should I cheat?" she said.

He put his arm around her back and squeezed her shoulder. "I'm just teasing. You think Polina believes all this nonsense? Putting lights on timers, twisting out the bulb in the
refrigerator? I've called her Saturdays and her phone has
been *busy*. She dials her mother as soon as Ben goes to shul.
Polina does what's best for Polina."

"I don't know," Gulia said. She'd noticed recently that
Vlad's talk could take a sudden cynical turn, which later he'd
claim was just a joke. Maybe, she wagered, he had been in love
with Polina when they were teenagers back in Vilnius, before
they'd come to this country. It seemed unlikely, but whatever

fellowship they'd once kept was evidently not the same now that Polina had chosen a skinny, yeshiva-boy lawyer over Vlad and his wit.

"Does she give you every Sunday off?" he asked, taking Gulia's hand familiarly and slipping their interlocked fingers into the pocket of his khakis. Of course her complicity had encouraged this. In the final minutes of their last date, Vlad had flagged her a taxi and, in the moment it took for the cab to pull up, had caught her unaware in what she remembered now less as a kiss than as a lunge. A lunge-kiss that had actually caused her to tip her head back to avoid the force. She'd pulled away abruptly as soon as she'd felt his tongue in her mouth. But why had she allowed him to relieve his tense expectation? She understood that her motive was selfish: to have recoiled from him so early would have meant no more phone calls; she would not be strolling down this walkway today, lined with elms and oaks, with the sunlight filtering through the leaves, walking not by herself or with the baby but with an actual man. This fact was enough to make her feel like the park had been cleaned for her, its hedges clipped and its grass manicured for her benefit alone. To have your own adult moment like this, you practically needed to have a man beside you.

"Sunday or Saturday, whichever I need off, Polina is very understanding." She slipped her fingers carefully out of Vlad's pocket.

"She told me about your situation. I don't know how you stood it for so long."

Gulia shrugged. "My husband was good to me. Sometimes he was the one I felt sorry for."

"But it's disgusting really. I'm shocked it's not illegal to have two wives."

"It *is* illegal," she said. She didn't know why she felt defensive suddenly. "Everyone turns a blind eye," she added, more calmly. "It was not so open when I was growing up. People frowned on it. The Soviets would have punished it. But now it is like time is moving backward. This is how it used to be—there is the wife you marry for yourself, and the one you marry for your parents."

He shook his head with a paternal compassion.

"Why were you never married?" she asked. It didn't feel like a mean question with the warmth of the sun on their backs.

Vlad shrugged. "No luck. I lived with a woman off and on for ten years. She'd had a tough life. I felt sorry for her, her mother was schizophrenic." He waited for a sad nod of agreement from Gulia before continuing. "It's common for first-degree relatives to get symptoms, later in life. I realized it wasn't something I wanted to look forward to."

A huffing female jogger ran an arc around them, her T-shirt pasted to her rounded back. "Look at this," he pointed. "Training for war, right?"

Had he been worried his girlfriend would go crazy, like her mother, or that the illness might pass along to his children? Couldn't real love withstand these abstract mitigations? She wondered if he felt any remorse about stealing ten years from a woman's life.

The runner had disappeared into a cross path where two face painters sat at a collapsible card table, the woman dabbing a brush on a child's cheek while her partner reclined in a director's chair, surveying the passersby. From the look of faint contempt on the man's face, Gulia could tell the two were Russian. On one of the benches, a fashionable woman in her seventies sat grooming her giant setter, pushing a brush through its sleek russet coat as lovingly as if it were the hair of a little girl. It seemed that people in the park were always tending to their animals as if they were children. She had yet to see a stray dog sleeping in the dust as she'd seen in Fergana, gazing up at you with yellowed, vinegary eyes. Vlad was leaning in close enough for her to smell his sharp, aquatic cologne. "I thought you'd like it," he whispered, as if this whole tucked-away stage life of the park was his doing.

Now that the face painters' table was free of children, the couple had lit up Winstons. A trace of warm dough drifted in between the odor of their tobacco. "Hungry?" Vlad said. He lifted his chin in the direction of a pretzel cart just off the path. Gulia shook her head.

He started off toward the cart with his slouchy gait. She *was* hungry, she realized, though not for anything from a pretzel stand. On the way to the park, she and Vlad had passed two or three restaurants that evidently were not up to his standards. She'd waited on the sidewalk while he studied the menus in the windows, concluding each time that the place wasn't for them. He'd taken her, in the end, up to the empty second floor of a Korean salad bar, where she'd grazed at her salad of sliced cucumbers, olives, and shredded carrots and eaten only the canned peaches. It wasn't that he was trying to take a shortcut on her, she thought; it was probably just part of Vlad's personality, the way extravagance was part of Rashid's. Even before Rashid had made his money on rugs, while they'd still lived modestly, he'd brought home the best fruit by the crateload. If she asked him to pick up a tube of toothpaste, he'd come back with three. Buying just one of anything was an embarrassment for him. His mistake had been to think this would keep her with him. The day he'd driven to pick her up from the airport, after her interview at the embassy in Tashkent, Layli had been sitting up front in his Mercedes, the two of them in oddly good spirits. On the ride back Rashid had detoured through one of Tashkent's posh new neighborhoods, where laborers squatted, laying bricks around the driveways of unfinished mansions. A few of them lifted their sun-baked heads when Rashid parked the car and clicked the automatic locks. At the end of the drive-way had stood a two-story idyll in white stucco, a steel balustrade around its marble terrace. Inside, they were greeted by a double staircase and marble floors and, in the back, a walled-off rose garden with a fountain. "Do you see all this?" Rashid had said to Layli. "Do you like it, my daugh-ter? You tell your mother to say no to America, I'll buy you this house tomorrow and sign it over in your name." Layli had giggled, not saying anything for Gulia's sake.

How could Rashid have thought a house would make her change her mind? She'd rather have had him shake her and slap her, make threats. But he was not so strong-willed. He loved her, but it was a resigned love, something he believed he could negotiate around.

Vlad returned, carrying a pretzel for himself and a Fanta for Gulia. With a hand on her lower back, he guided her down the walkway to the big grass field swarming with people. There was a spicy, hay-scented smell of mowed grass being cooked in the sun, a game going on between shirtless young men chasing a flying disk and a team still wearing their clothes. People sat on blankets or in the shadows of trees, be-side their overturned bicycles, oblivious to the city around them. She and Vlad walked on the outside of the shallow net fencing that encircled the lawn until they were on a shadier walkway heading uphill between boulders on which mangier shirtless men dozed. Vlad removed his citigroup cap and dabbed the sweat off his forehead with his arm; he looked at Gulia with amorous, heavy-lidded eyes and smiled exhaustedly. His expression reminded her of a house dog's, waiting for what it was entitled to out of loyalty and affection.

"I'm going to Fire Island next weekend," he said. He studied her face to determine if she knew what he was talking about. "It's off of Long Island. It's the one where everybody leaves their cars on the dock and takes the ferry."

She thought of guests removing their shoes before entering a house.

"My friends rent a cottage there. I thought you'd like to get out of the city next weekend."

Did a cottage mean he expected her to stay overnight, share his room? Please, *please* ask someone else, she wanted to say. *I know nothing about these sorts of things.*

"I wanted to buy clothes for my daughter next weekend," she said.

Vlad picked a little salt off his pretzel. "I guess that's important." His eyes scanned around, ostensibly for one of the exit gates. "Do what you need to do," he said, all business now.

Half an hour ago she had recoiled from taking his hand. Now his attention seemed too precious, too unfamiliar to risk losing as quickly as she'd won it. "I'll find time to buy her something earlier in the week," Gulia said, with a face she hoped was cheerful.

Gulia's phone launched into its refrain of *Carmen* while she applied a second coat of color to her nails. She'd laid Yoni down for his nap twenty minutes earlier and retrieved the polish from under the kitchen sink, where she'd forgotten it after buying it her first week at Polina's. She'd chosen a dragon lady color to dot the handles of the meat pots and meat utensils, in order to tell them apart from the dairy, a brazen red she'd never consider wearing. But now such reservations seemed prudish and silly. In a city where no one cared anyway, why hide oneself away like some invalid? The *Carmen* overture was still playing, going on its third loop now. She waved her fingers to dry them and picked up the phone.

"Asal?"

"Rashid, how nice of you to call," she said. "Five days, I was about to give up on you."

He didn't bother answering. "Tell your lady doctor to find a new maid," he said. "I'm divorcing Nasrin."

Her elbow knocked the nail polish over and spilled a pool on the newsprint. A heated prickle was spreading down her arms.

"Don't fool me anymore, Rashid."

"Are you listening to me? God has looked favorably on us. I found her an apartment in town so she can visit the children."

"She's not taking them?"

"They're staying where they belong, Gulia. In the house with the family. My mother and sister will look after them."

"She agreed?" An idiotic question.

"That's how it's been decided."

As though she'd forgotten that, were it not for Morad's drug problem, she most likely wouldn't have kept Layli.

"Better I return Nasrin to her parents, right? In disgrace. *Take your daughter back. We don't need her anymore.* At least I'll save her that scandal, pardon me!" He sounded stunned by what he had done, by what she had made him do. "Do you have any idea what people are saying, Gulia?"

She listened silently.

"Say something!" he demanded.

"I don't know what to say."

It was as though he were offering her a big, expensive gift and all he wanted in return was a mindless giddiness, anything to make him forget how much the gift had cost.

"Then kiss me," he said.

"How am I going to kiss you over the phone?"

"Kiss me!"

And this time she did as he asked, pressing her lips to the raised keypad on the phone.

They were seated at an outdoor table that gave Gulia a clear view of the inside of the restaurant. The walls of the dining room were covered with sepia posters of old American films, distantly familiar images of *Casablanca* and *Gone with the Wind*, the face of a young Omar Sharif as Doctor Zhivago.

"You know who that one is," Vlad said, pointing with his fork.

"I don't know."

He had named all the actors he'd recognized so far, presumably for her benefit.

"Yes, you do. *The Christ-father*." He appeared both shocked and pleased with her ignorance. "Marlon Brando!"

Gulia poked her fork around the slippery tangerine slice at the lip of her plate. She wanted to measure her words carefully, but her face was probably broadcasting everything.

They'd been talking about Fire Island again, about the gays who summered there, who'd made themselves the gatekeepers of real estate, according to Vlad, and were the reason the rentals were getting so expensive every year.

"Vlad, I can't go," she said, looking up at him. "Thank you for asking me, but it wouldn't be fair. I am returning to Fergana."

Vlad swallowed down what must have been the last piece of food in his mouth and wiped his lip with the corner of the napkin.

"My husband is leaving the woman who . . ." She did not know what to call Nasrin now. "The woman," she said, simply.

All day it had been her secret. She had told no one so far. "He's been very troubled since I left."

"I'm sure he has," Vlad wiped his mouth again. "Wow. It's some story. I didn't know you still spoke to him."

"We are not enemies."

"Uhhm." He gazed at the boat of sugar packets between them. "You aren't enemies. Haha. I like that. Amiable arbitration." He gave her a rueful smile. "Isn't that the key to negotiation?"

"What?" she said.

"Showing you can walk away."

She regarded him for a moment but couldn't think of what he was talking about.

"I'm just curious," he said. "Why come here? Why not go to New Zealand or Tahiti, somewhere exotic to wait it out and indulge in stories of your old life?"

He *was* cynical, she thought, cynical and self-pitying. It was horrible to think how close she had come to being with him.

"I heard once," she said, "that it is in how people part ways that we learn the most about them."

Vlad grinned at some private thought and picked something out of his teeth as if she weren't there. "I wish you
luck," he said, with no affect.

"You, as well."

They seemed to run out of words then and fell into a
sober silence, during which a honking taxi stalled and finally
rolled past. She watched the people strolling on the other
side of the canvas partition. A few looked like tourists; those
she thought were New Yorkers looked well groomed, certain
of themselves, but also preoccupied and worn down. Within
a few moments, their waiter was at the table, offering tea and
dessert that they both declined.

She'd knocked herself out with the aid of two valerian capsules
and in her subterranean sleep had glimpsed the old alley where
she'd walked a hundred times, where men squatted over
backgammon boards. It was a familiar, anxious tune that woke
her up, fracturing the fragile trance of her dream, the cursed
theme from *Carmen*, and when she opened her eyes, a blinking
red light reflected in the empty water glass on her nightstand.

"Gulnara, are you up?" It was her aunt's voice, as low as a
man's.

"Yes, what's wrong?" She squinted in the dark at the
night-shining sky in the window. "Is it Layli?"

"No. Our girl is fine. It's Nasrin."

Gulia got out of bed and felt around for her slippers.

"Rashid's Nasrin," her aunt said, in response to Gulia's
silence. "She carried a kerosene lamp into their courtyard
last night and poured it all over herself. Then she struck a
match. The neighbor just came and told us."

"Kerosene?" The words were arranging themselves into a strange constellation in her head.

"Yes, the ambulance came. Everybody could hear her screaming on the street. They say it's because Rashid was tossing her out."

"Who said that?" Gulia felt feverish. She took a step toward Yoni's crib. His cheek was pressed to the sheet, his blanket tossed aside.

"Now people are calling me, asking if Rashid was throwing her out because you are coming back," her aunt said.

"He was not *throwing* her out, Auntie. He bought her an apartment."

"Then you *knew*? This is all true, what I hear about you from strangers?"

Gulia stared out at the transparent night. A few lights were already on in the sleeping apartment buildings. The Queensboro Bridge was still suspended over the dark river, and somewhere in the world tongues were already flapping.

She took the elevator down to the lobby so she wouldn't wake anyone when she called Rashid. It was six in the morning, and in the corridor behind the reception table, a few doctors were picking up their mail, straggling in from a sleepless night.

She lowered herself onto the leather couch and listened to Rashid tell her that Nasrin was still alive.

"Now you will never leave her," she said.

"It is in God's hands."

Her arms and the top of her chest had been burned badly, he said, almost down to the muscle. He'd been asleep, in another room of the house, he added. Screams from the out-side had woken up the whole house, and by the time he ran into the fenced-in courtyard where they kept the car, flames were leaping from her nightgown. He'd put them out by wrapping her in a carpet hanging on the railing of the porch. She was still delirious when the ambulance arrived, he said, begging him to kill her.

Gulia listened silently. There was still sand in her eyes from her herb-induced sleep. The doctors were gone, and she was alone again in the centrally cooled lobby where the only other living creatures were two potted palms by the doors. She tried not to imagine Nasrin, walking into the courtyard, guided by the lamp that would soon bathe her in fire. It wasn't despair that had made Nasrin do it, she thought, it was simple vengeance. How did one compete with insanity? she wondered. Whatever pain and hopelessness she'd felt herself, she could never raise them to a level of such violence.

"What do you want me to do now?" she said finally. "Come back to you while you sit at her bedside?"

"We need to wait, Gulia. Can't you wait?"

"Oh yes, and how the years go by."

She felt sorry for making this more difficult for him now. Surely his pain was something she couldn't understand. He was living a nightmare, had been living it for years by split-ting himself in two. She wondered if a part of him loved Nas-rin. She had no idea anymore. Rashid was like the moon: the side of him that faced Nasrin was eternally in shadow.

"Gulia, we can't lose our hope."

"Hoping is hard work," she said. She thought back to her life, living in that house with Morad and his parents, her only salvation the rotary phone in the hallway. It would ring for her after midnight, when everybody had gone upstairs to sleep and she was still awake, rinsing Layli's linens and hand-washing the entire house's laundry. She would shake the water off her hands and run to pick up before the second ring. At twenty she might have tried killing herself too, if it had not been for Rashid's late-night phone calls.

But what hope could they speak of now? she wondered. That Nasrin would not survive what she had done to herself? Even if they moved to Tashkent, where no one knew them, could they still look into each other's eyes after this?

"Gulia, I don't know what to do. I have no one else on my side besides you." His voice had risen steadily until it sounded like a sob. She felt her own chest swell, her throat stiffen. Eleven years ago she'd held her breath until he spoke the code word they'd agreed on, *"Taxi?"* in case someone else in the house picked up. A whole affair carried on in secret, even though they hadn't so much as kissed.

"Asal, are you still there?"

She watched two young doctors walk in through the doors, pausing their dialogue to glance at her. Their expressions changed into grimaces—professional instincts that registered pain and disturbance. What was written on her face, she wondered, that would make them look at her like this?

"I'm still here."

"We must ask God to help us," Rashid said.

She looked up and caught the eye of one of the doctors glancing back at her as he stepped into the elevator. She swallowed the mucus in the back of her throat. They were so worried here about appearing intrusive, she thought. Everything was the opposite of Fergana, but she could get used to it.

"We must ask God for help, together," he repeated in a low tone.

"It might be time," she said. "It might be time that you and I started asking God for different things."

Gulia waited for him to speak, but he didn't. She laid the phone down on the red leather, letting Rashid end their call. Her arms shivered from sitting too long in the extreme air conditioning. She folded them tightly across her chest and looked through the doors, at the sky holding its first yellow. She could see the corner of a fenced-off construction area, the view of a crane obstructed by the lobby's ceiling. It was morning, and the neighborhood was becoming familiar again.

BETTER HALF

THEY WERE BOTH TWENTY-TWO and married ten months. Anya couldn't remember what half their fights were about anymore, those ongoing, line-crossing attacks. One day Ryan had called her a slut for leaving the apartment in only her long T-shirt. (She'd gone downstairs to get the mail.) Another night it was the scent of trout in the apartment, which he claimed stank up his clothes. He didn't want to walk into people's houses and move their furniture smelling like the seafood section. This time they'd argued about the loose change, the dimes and pennies Ryan excavated out of his jeans and left all over the place, instead of dropping them into the glass jar on the counter that she'd set out for just that purpose. That's why, she said, he and his friends were going to still be buying scratch-off tickets when they were fifty.

That had been going too far, she knew. But Ryan took it even further, grabbing the glass jar off the counter and tossing it with a heavy dead pitch at the wall behind her head. It crashed a foot from where Anya stood, shattering glass and spilling change.

"What are you, crazy?" she yelled. "Are you nuts!"

The pennies and dimes were rolling under the radiator, behind the cabinets.

"Bitch doesn't shut up," he said, starting off toward the door.

Ten months earlier they'd driven to the county court-house in White Plains, just two weeks after Anya's mother had called from Dolsk to say her father was recovering from a heart attack. Soon he'd be taken to Nizhniy Novgorod for surgery, was what her mother said, in an optimistic tone cal-culated not to scare her. But the news filled Anya with a throat-closing panic, a fear of time and its consequences. She hadn't seen her parents in a year and might not for an-other two or three, depending on how things went for her here. It was time to ask for a favor: marry now and sort out their feelings later.

She'd expected the hard part would be getting Ryan to agree, to offer something more than an ambivalent moan. But to watch him get down on one knee three days later to propose in earnest (because she was his Russian queen, his pot of gold, and doing it halfway was no way), this she hadn't bargained for.

Stepping over the glass shards, Anya walked to the window in time to catch the reddish-brown top of Ryan's head. He was cutting across the parking lot, heading toward his old hatchback Tracer. Only two places for him to go, she knew, the Bull & Brew or his mamma's. She watched the car shud-der to a start, then make a wide, sloppy turn into the road be-fore it was gone. There was nothing left to do now but fetch the broom and dustpan from behind the refrigerator and to think about what she was going to say tomorrow when she went to see Erin, her lawyer.

The first time her mother had asked about Ryan's family on the phone, all Anya could think to tell her was "his mother goes to church." There was no reason to say the rest, that no father was around to speak of, that the brother was a degenerate gambler who'd spent two years as a guest of New York State. She did not say that Ryan's mother hadn't come to the courthouse, and that his brother had only shown up later at the Bull & Brew, where all of Ryan's friends had come to toast the newlyweds and get properly obliterated.

She was already in bed when Ryan's key scratched in the lock. She could hear the door undo in little creaks. Then he was drawing it closed behind him, gently so as not to wake her. For a moment it was quiet, but she could sense his stiff, lumbering presence in the doorway of their bedroom.

"Either come in or take your pillow to the couch," she said in the dark, faking a sleepy hoarseness. "Just don't stand there and keep me awake."

He shucked off his pants and got in under the comforter in his T-shirt, shifting the weight of the bed.

"I hate you," she said, pressing her cold feet to his calves.

"Stop it. What are you doing . . . ?"

"I'm freezing."

He wrapped his arm around her.

"You could have killed me," she said.

He dipped his hand under her nightgown and cupped the warm roll of her stomach. "No way, I got better aim than that."

"Are you sorry?"

"Mmmhmm." His hand slid up higher and greeted her breast with a loyal squeeze. She drew it away. There would be no rewards tonight for trying to kill her. He seemed not to notice her rebuff and only pressed in closer, like a child. Sometimes it was easier to see him as a child who got all his power from being unpredictable and erratic. Her mother had once described some men this way—husbands of women who came to her clinic with their lips busted up like boxers, or who'd had their faces wiped in the same vomit they'd refused to clean up. Ryan wasn't that demented, though he found other ways to torment her, like coming into the diner a whole hour before the end of her shift, just to sit at the bar and watch her serve customers. Beside her Ryan's body jerked in a little spasm of sleep, and he drew her in closer. *His pot of gold.* Did he even *hear* himself? "You love me," he'd told her the second night they'd spent together. She thought he'd been kidding, but then he'd said, "You do. If I died tomorrow, you'd come to my funeral and say you loved me." "Don't say things like that," she'd scolded, while a fat tear slid down her cheek. Maybe she really did love him that time. After all, who else was there to?

She'd taken the train home from Nizhniy Novgorod right after her exams, worried that her parents would think her plan frivolous. It was the end of her third winter semester, and she was coming to ask them for money to go to Maine; the university had contacts at hotels in Kennebunkport, a town whose very name—chirped by the girls in her English class who'd worked there the previous summer—sounded spry and upbeat in its foreignness. Her parents, it turned out, needed no convincing. They seemed happy to let her go and see the brighter surface of life before its grayer truths set in. That night, having her father's promise to pay for airfare, she went out with her two childhood girlfriends, one of them already divorced. At a party they tossed their empty bottles off the balcony onto the roofs of the tin garages below, howling. On Sunday morning before going back to Nizhniy Novgorod, she went with her mother to the market, where next to the meat pavilion old men were selling their war medals. A hole. It was the only way Anya could think of Dolsk since she'd started college. You had to know these holes. Sooner or later they closed in around you.

Never could she have dreamed up a place as beguilingly small as Kennebunkport, a fishing village made over into a sovereignty of yachts and jewelry shops. The restaurant where she washed dishes faced a marina. On her breaks she could go out the back to have a smoke and watch the bobbing boats, their nodding masts set off against an eerie confluence of glistening water and dull sky. Even on the most sweltering days, there was a breeze to cool her sweat while she drew on the menthol.

The room she shared with three other girls was in a guest-house belonging to the couple who owned the restaurant, and almost all the money she'd made in the kitchen had gone right back to them in rent. She'd noted the convenience of this arrangement to one of her roommates, a self-important twit who'd replied that the point of their trip was not to make money but to see the world. But August was half over, and what had she seen? Only the kitchen and stretches of Route 9 at night. High grass fields and parked speedboats, passing quickly in the window of the assistant cook's car whenever James took them on their midnight runs for liquor and ice cream. Every Tuesday, after the last trays of dishes were run through the Hobart, they'd all meet on his porch to drink, and it was on one of these nights that Anya finally asked James whether any of the girls ever stayed past the summer.

"Anya's always thinking of something," he said delinquently.

All season she'd found James's ponytail and overuse of her name to be on the lecherous side of friendly. She'd fallen for both early on, and all that had stopped her from going to bed with him was the fact that one or another of the work-travel girls was always willing to stay later at his parties. It was her provincial pride, she thought, that didn't sit well with giving in to such passive motives in a man. In her heart she still believed in being pursued. She was glad of it now, leaning against the posts of his porch and lighting her cigarette off his in the sharp, salty wind. He seemed pleased to be invited finally into some transgression, one of a deeper sort than sex. He offered Anya a ride to New York City but told her she'd have a tough time there with rent. His friend's sister managed a diner in Kitchawank Hills, he said, a rich commuter town named after an imaginary Indian chief. At the end of August, he drove Anya to meet Alexis, the manager, who resembled a goalie on a women's hockey team and who looked at Anya like a farmer sizing up a mare and asked her if she had a Social Security card. There was only one way to answer this question, and James had already reassured her that Alexis wouldn't ask to see it.

The diner started her on the slower afternoon shifts, and for a while Anya had the evenings to herself. From the mattress on the floor of her efficiency, she watched TV on an old set that Nick, another waiter, had given her. Nick had taken it upon himself to "train" her, which meant that she now had to abide his criticism and his daily reminders to *smile*, and also to endure the unpleasant surprises of having him walk up from behind to massage her shoulders, though all of this was worth tolerating for the car rides back to her low-rise, a mile and a half uphill. It was better, she knew, to work the front of the restaurant and not complain, than to be stuck in the kitchen with the Ecuadorians and Guatemalans, who, after five or six years in Kitchawank Hills, spoke worse English than she did and seemed to have no life outside of the restaurant, talking always about who was, and was not, to be trusted there.

The kitchen's goings-on made their way to Anya through Berenice, the restaurant's lone Salvadorian. Bernice was twenty-four but looked forty and in her confessional paranoia liked to warn Anya about the Guatemalans, who could bring you a home-cooked meal one day and try to get you fired the next. She had ridden through their sorry mountainous country, she said, and then across Mexico, on a bus with a stench she would not soon forget, where everyone had worn diapers and not been let out to use the bathroom for three days. Every piece of gossip Berenice relayed seemed to have a single point: that trying to escape your tedious fate only led you back to it. Her favorite example of this was one of the cooks, a handsome boy named Sergio, who had started working out at the gym where his cousin washed the towels. Sergio had found himself a rich divorced lady there, but the lady had turned out to be nothing but more work. Now all he ever did was grumble when she called and asked him to come over, since he usually ended up chopping her wood or repairing little things around her big house. He talked of going to nightclubs to meet girls, even though everyone knew he was too scared to step into a club, get his fake ID taken away, and be deported.

In November Anya picked up the dinner shifts and served whomever the other waiters ignored, high school kids after basketball games, mommies who ordered nothing but salad and crackers for their kids to crush, and the Retard Party, which was what Nick called Ryan and his friends when they came in one snowy Thursday night and made a nuisance of themselves by shaking salt out on their tabletop and drawing pictures in it with their fingers. "Yo, take this water away," one of them called to a waiter. "I'm thirsty, not dirty!"

They made Anya read the specials twice, grinning like monkeys. When she returned with their food, another of them tapped her shoulder and pointed at the smirky, big-shouldered guy across the table. "Will you kiss Ry-Ry?" he said. "It's his birthday." She'd turned to Ryan with a mur-derous look, but he was blushing fiercely under his New York Rangers cap. "I apologize for these scumbags," he'd said. Later she'd tell him she'd only been nice because he looked like the most nervous person at the table. But it wasn't true. She'd wanted to stand there a little longer, suddenly the cen-ter of all the fuss. They had tried so hard to get her attention, having no idea that she was so lonely.

Erin's degrees hung framed on the exposed brick wall, between her bookcase and black file cabinet. There were few personal touches in her office, Anya had noticed. No pictures of a hus-band or children, or dogs. Only a Beanie Bear with a tennis racket sitting atop her bound legal volumes, and a potted or-chid on her desk, as stiff-spined and pale as Erin herself.

"How is your father?" Erin said. She didn't look up from her papers.

"He's better. He has pains when he walks, and he takes lots of aspirin, but he's waiting for . . ."

Erin nodded without looking up, probably not listening. She had the face of a neat bird. Her hair was pulled back from her square, somewhat manly forehead. She looked to Anya like a girl who'd been a good student all her life by working hard, even at things that were easy.

"That's good. You may get to see him very soon," Erin said absentmindedly. It was the same thing she'd said the first time Anya had come into her office, right after she and Ryan were married and Anya had wanted to start applying for her resident papers.

Now Anya ran her finger along the edge of a wooden plaque on Erin's desk. *Each time a man stands up for an ideal or acts to improve the lot of others or strikes out against injustice, he sends a tiny ripple of hope* . . . The first time she'd read it, Anya had asked Erin who had spoken these words. Bobby Kennedy, Erin had said, and added that the Kennedys had done more on behalf of poor people in this country than almost anyone else. So, Erin liked poor people.

Erin's parents, Anya had learned, were a schoolteacher and a school librarian, a fact that had initially made Anya decide that she liked Erin. It seemed to suggest that becoming a lawyer hadn't been an expectation for her but a certain kind of generational progress, or at least the mindful choice of one life over another. The first few times in Erin's office, she'd felt eager to get her advice, to ask if she should transfer her credits and complete her linguistics degree, or start over in something more practical. But such discussions had turned out to be difficult to strike up, with Erin always looking at the clock, or taking phone calls, and never asking Anya any questions other than the necessary ones.

"Where's Ryan?" Erin said.

Anya removed her finger from the plaque. "At work."

"Didn't you say he was coming with you?"

Anya lifted her shoulders in an ignorant shrug. Today they were supposed to get prepped for their marriage interview. But after Ryan's jar-throwing the night before, she'd let him leave the house without reminding him.

"Look, Anya, you're the one who needs this," Erin said. She slid a sheet across the desk. It was a list of questions Anya and Ryan might get asked: how both of them liked their coffee, the title of the last movie they'd seen together, the names of their parents.

Anya read through the list silently. "What if he doesn't remember my parents' names?"

"He doesn't have to know everything. It's better if there's a mistake."

"What if he messes up on purpose?"

"*Why* would he do that?"

Just *because*, Anya felt like saying. She had never been able to have a serious talk with Ryan about this whole . . . process. Every time she tried, he'd start singing some rap tune (. . . *how long will ya mourn me!*) and then he'd tell her to *relax*, which she had begun to think of as the most retarded word in the English language.

Erin leafed through her desk calendar. "You still have time to prepare. The interview might be in two months from now, or it might be a year from now."

"If we're still married in a year."

Erin frowned. "Be careful with divorce. It's going to really complicate things."

"I *am* careful. *He's* the one who's always saying he doesn't trust me! He threw a glass jar full of coins at me last night. I'm lucky I'm alive."

Erin's blue eyes were frozen in uncertainty. She took her time answering. "Anya, if you're worried about this. I mean, if you can *show* it's a problem, then you can probably find a way to self-petition." Her voice had dropped, not exactly to a whisper, but to a low tone that was more genuinely concerned, more shrewd than any Anya had heard her use before. "He wouldn't have anything to do with the process," she added reassuringly.

Anya lowered her eyes to the wooden plaque again. "At all?" she asked, to be certain.

The apartment she and Ryan had moved into the previous February sat above a bridal shop on an outlying stretch of Main Street that turned into a through road. In the shop display the mannequins who posed in mawkish and badly sewn gowns stood under a banner advertising "Communion Dresses and Veils." But by December the banner was gone, replaced with dangling stars and tinsel, the same tinsel that had been stuck to the windows of the diner. At home she would have been finishing up her second-to-last semester, Anya thought, getting ready to take a train home for a few days, where her mother would be waiting for her on the platform, waving madly.

Alexis was closing the restaurant early for the Christmas Party. She'd gone to each of them individually with a pen and legal pad beforehand, to "get a commitment." By the time Anya and Ryan arrived that evening, everyone who was going to show up was already there, playing a game involving Twizzlers, while Alexis shouted "Sucker!" from the end of a table loaded with food and liquor bottles. She was soused. Most of them were. She screamed at Nick when a half-chewed Twizzler fell out of his mouth. A Twizzler game without hands, it looked like. Around the table the faces were slick with sweat, or red from sucking. The faces of galley slaves.

Nick, out of the game now, found her an empty chair while Ryan hunted for his own. Soon a game of drink-or-dare was begun, with Alexis giving the commands again, instructing a pot washer named Luis to recite a tongue-twister about seashells by the seashore. He mangled it, as expected, to a round of convulsive laughter, and looked glad finally to toss back a drink in the peace of his defeat.

When Berenice's turn came, she was ordered to stand with her back to the wall and bend backward to kiss it. She arched her spine slowly, trying to stay balanced, oblivious to the display she was giving of her deep breasts spread out and flattened under her Lycra shirt. After the noise died down, Alexis scanned the table, giving each of them a speculative glance. She pulled a long string of licorice out of the sack on the table and twirled it in her fingers, then tossed it to Nick. "One end goes in your mouth," she instructed, and turned her gummy smile at Anya. "Help him out, honey."

There was a light drumbeat of fists on the table, and some anonymous kissing noises, which didn't escape Ryan. He was bent over his whiskey glass, next to her, looking revolted. She smoothed down his hair. There was something almost endearing about seeing him suffer so stupidly over a party game. She stuck the Twizzler in her mouth and closed her eyes so she wouldn't have to look into Nick's fat, tanned face. The air in the room was as stifling as a kennel. She could hear Nick's moist chewing sounds on the other end of the licorice, which tasted like leather in her mouth. He smelled not just of drink but of fermentation. She felt the warm, acrid breath too close to her face and bit off.

"Hey, peace in the Middle East, man," Nick said afterward, trying to pour Ryan a drink.

"You're standing a little too close, so how about you move the fuck away," Ryan answered, a vein showing through his temple. Nick moved back to a respectful distance, and his mouth formed the helpless grin of a shit-eater. It was time for all of them to start heading home.

She was still trying to latch her seatbelt when the car lurched backward. The interior smelled of alcohol, coming off in hot waves from Ryan's skin. The Tracer backed out onto the road like a rocket, with a sharp jolting turn, then raced forward.

"Slow down," she whispered. In the side-view mirror the diner's sign was receding quickly into a small neon rectangle. Ahead of them the light switched from yellow to red like a blinking eye while Ryan ran the dark intersection.

Anya sat stiffly in her seat.

"Watch the road, Ryan."

"You watch yourself."

She didn't answer.

"You like toying with me?"

The best thing to say was nothing.

"Scheming bitch."

"Scheming! What would I be scheming about? You're always coming to the diner to *spy* on me. Anything I ever did, you know about."

"Lining up a boyfriend."

"If your drunk ass gets pulled over right now, my 'boyfriend' is who's gonna be giving me rides to work."

He floored the brake and sent her flying forward, her nose a centimeter from the glove compartment before her body slammed back against the seat. The car skidded sideways and came to a stop in the center of the lanes. Suddenly the lights were off completely.

"Always playing stupid."

"No one can see the car! Turn the lights on before some-one kills us!"

She moved for the door and heard the hard click of the automatic lock. A pair of headlights behind them was getting brighter.

"He's laying it on me every day in the men's room!" The car was closing in, its beams illuminating their cloth-seat up-holstery. "Now move!" she shouted.

Ryan switched on the headlights, and the speeding lights behind them veered left with an earsplitting shriek of rubber. Someone was yelling "Assholes!" out the window while honk-ing. An accelerator was ripping back into high gear.

"Fuck you!" Ryan shouted as the other car drove away.

Anya leaned back and breathed heavily. It was a miracle that the other lane had been empty. Their Tracer was rolling again, cruising down the street in dead silence. They were on the main drag of shops, passing a shoe store and a beauty sa-lon with giant faces pasted in the window. Ryan slowed down and pulled over to the curb. "Now get the hell out of my car," he said as the door locks unclicked. "Your fat ass isn't getting a free ride no more."

"Fool," she muttered, stepping out. She tried to slam the door, but her purse got caught, and the door closed by itself with a light slap. A draft of icy air stunned her thighs. She'd worn the thin velveteen dress she'd hemmed that morning, so foolishly, above the knee. The Tracer rounded the next corner, and soon the rumble of its engine was gone, replaced only by a ringing winter silence.

A skirt of crusted snow fringed the sidewalk. Anya zipped her wool jacket up to her chin and started walking. She tucked her fingers into her armpits and then nearly slipped on a patch of ice. She couldn't see a single restaurant or bar from which to call a cab. Stores, stores, stores: a Sam Goody, a Payless, all locked up. She licked her tongue along her chapped bottom lip and tasted the ferrous tang of blood. From far off echoed the howl of a train horn, a sonorous, unhuman wail. She could hear the sound of a car from behind. She stopped walking and turned around. Ryan was back. She waited for him to pull up, but the car slowed without getting any closer to the curb. She stepped off the sidewalk, but he sped up again.

"Now who's the fool!" he shouted through the open window, his voice cutting through the soundless air.

Anya pulled a cold hand out of her armpit and flipped him the finger. "Go make another circle around the block, idiot!"

"Keep walking, fool!" he yelled, pressing the gas.

She walked on ahead, tucking her chin into her chest to hide from the driving wind. How she hated him! To think he'd driven back just to torment her. She could rip up her vocal cords yelling or ignore him; it didn't matter, he'd find a way to make her suffer. How had she ended up here, alone at one in the morning on an empty sidewalk, unable to feel her hands or face? Just a few nights ago she had dreamed that her parents had come to Kitchawank Hills to take her home. Now she wanted to laugh—she'd never go home. Not to that

dreary, snowed-in remoteness, not to her shabby water-
damaged dorm in Nizhniy Novgorod, not to a life where her
mother spent summers tending tomato patches that she'd
been planting for twenty years, and canning those same
tomatoes out of some primitive memory of need. She didn't
want to go back to where everything was either unfinished or
deteriorating.

She maneuvered ahead, the cold dragging her lungs. Far,
far off wailed the siren of an emergency vehicle. The wind
seemed to have subsided. Just ahead Anya could see an ATM
and beside it, like a mirage, a pay phone.

The cab delivered her to the dimmed display of the bridal
shop. Their living room window upstairs was lit up. Anya
climbed the enclosed stairwell to find the door of the apartment unlocked. The chaos was obvious before she pushed it
open all the way. Her hair clips, tweezers, loose cigarettes,
cough drops, poker chips, all flung out onto the stained carpet. Ryan was sitting on their old plaid sofa, watching a basketball game. He didn't bother to turn when she walked in.
"Who's cleaning this up, huh?" she said.

No answer from the couch.

His short clay pipe lay on its little foil coaster on the coffee table. He'd moved it aside to the corner of the table to
put up his feet. Instead of the usual pungent odor of his pot,
the room smelled of her perfume samples, which he'd evidently also tossed onto the floor. He'd become too lazy to
even bother stashing his herb and pipe when he wasn't smoking the stuff. She walked over to the dresser, where the top
drawer had been pulled open. Except for the daisy-printed
vinyl lining, it was completely empty.

"Where are my working papers?" she said.

Ryan turned up the volume.

"They were here in a Ziploc bag!"

"You'll get them back when I trust you."

She walked to the couch and blocked the TV. "Where'd you put them?"

He tried to swat her away. "Get out of my face, woman."

"They're *my* goddamn papers!"

"Yours? They aren't *yours.* You never would've gotten them without me. You got *nothing* here without me."

She went for the collar of his T-shirt, but he pushed her away. She clubbed him hard in the ear.

"Bitch!" He tucked his ear into his shoulder. It wasn't clear if he was cursing at her or at the pain.

"You deserve it," she said nervously.

He grabbed her arm in a wristlock. She tried to twist free, but there was more strength in his hand than he was using.

"You think everyone owes you something?" he said, and shoved her backward on the couch.

She reached for his arm and dug her nails into the fabric. "Shit-for-brain *loser.*" His palm was in her face, pushing her down again. "Born through the ass!" she muttered. Her leg sprang up in a badly aimed kick at his middle, making Ryan stagger backward. He scrabbled for a foothold, waltzing forward with his arm bent up. And that's when it came, the blind, bulldozing pain shooting through the bridge of her nose into her eyes, and spreading in a strange, paralyzing heat around her face.

The side of her forehead hit the carpet. She heard the thud of her own skull as her head met the floor. A slick, metallic taste of blood was on her tongue, mixed with the coarse fuzz of carpet fibers and hair. She gagged, trying to spit them out, as the TV droned on in the background.

When she opened her eyes, Ryan was standing over her. She palmed around for the side of the couch and tried to use it to sit up. She felt Ryan's hand touching her shoulder, trying to help.

"Get away from me." Anya sat up and closed her eyes against the stabbing pain. She wiped her lip with her arm. "Look what you did!" She dipped her head back and cupped her nose, catching drops of dark blood in her palm. She felt dizzy.

"Why'd you stick your face under my elbow?"

"Shut up!" She looked at the red streak on her arm. "Mmm. My *lip*."

"Your lip was bleeding when you came in."

She got up and hobbled to the bathroom, while Ryan followed behind. He stopped just short of the door as she leaned into the mirror and examined the marks on her face. It looked like someone had rubbed her chin with rope. There was fresh blood under her nose. Her bottom lip had split down the middle, as she'd feared, in the spot where it had been chapped.

"Thanks a lot," she said. She ran the tap and patted her face with cold water. Ryan maundered back into the living room, looking for his shoes. She heard the jingle of the key chain. "Thanks a lot for my face!" she shouted, as the door slammed behind him.

In the mirror, Anya examined her wet face, not quite recognizing the sneering, fanatical-looking creature. Her lip throbbed along to the pulse in her head. She slicked back her hair and wiped away the runny stamp of mascara under her right eye. She tried to soften her eyes into an empty catastrophic look, but the more determined expression wore its way through.

The living room looked like a post-atomic mess. Anya

picked up the remote control, which had fallen on the floor amid the debris of cards, crushed cigarettes, and loose tampons, and silenced the television. She took the clay pipe off the coffee table and rolled up the square of aluminum foil with the remains of Ryan's weed, then carried both into the kitchen, where a cereal box he hadn't put away stood on the counter. She shoved the pipe and marijuana deep into the rice puffs, then removed the phone from its cradle on the wall and punched in the police.

Sitting in the leather armchair and staring at Erin's diplomas on the brick wall, Anya felt a kind of numbing safety. It was like the safety of being in school, with its promise that everything could be done the one right way.

"Did you bring the signed affidavits?" Erin asked.

Anya pulled them out from a blue plastic folder. There was one from Alexis, attesting that her marriage to Ryan was genuine and that he was a familiar face around the diner. Before Anya had moved out of the apartment and into a room in a beat-up Victorian, she'd had her landlord write a statement confirming that she and Ryan had been "cohabitating." Erin already had a copy of the police report and a copy of Anya's order of protection, which she held up now.

"Do you want to go to court and make this permanent?"

"Do I need to?"

"It won't hurt your case."

"I don't know. He thinks I'm going to get the order lifted."

"And why would he think that?" Erin said. "Have you been *talking* to him?"

"No."

"That doesn't look good, Anya."

"I *know*."

"He's out of the picture or he's not."

Erin separated the original documents from the copies and gave a set back to Anya. "A restraining order means no phone chatting, no Valentine cards, no calling him if you have a leaky toilet . . ."

"I got it." Anya put the folder back in her bag and stood up.

"We'll talk in a couple of weeks, then," Erin said.

"Yeah."

The sky was already gray with twilight when Anya descended the narrow stairwell to the street. It got dark so early she hardly ever noticed the arrival of evenings anymore. She thought of walking the block to the diner and calling Ryan for a ride home but then remembered Erin's warning. It had been ridiculous to think she could speak to Erin openly, to delude herself that Erin was her friend. She had no real friends here, no one to whom she could explain that in the five weeks since the police had ordered Ryan to stay at least three hundred feet away from her, she'd felt his presence more than ever. If she worked on a Wednesday night, she'd hear from Berenice that Ryan had come in on Tuesday. If her shift was over at six, she'd learn that Ryan had walked in for a burger at a quarter to seven. She had even seen his car in the parking lot of the A&P when she'd gone out for groceries. He was out of the picture, all right. He was out of the picture just about every place she went.

And she had to admit that there were moments when she needed him, when she really did. Last Thursday had been one of them. She'd mixed up the entrées of two different tables, then spilled hollandaise sauce on a customer's pants trying to sort it out. She knew from the look on the man's face that there would be no tip, but she hadn't expected a "YOU SUCK" to be scrawled on the credit card slip he'd left behind. Then she'd had to put in another two hours at work, dragging herself around with a forced grin until eleven. Who wouldn't need a drink after that? She'd crossed the half-lit parking lot and entered the Bull & Brew at its side door, where the pinball machines and video games stood. She'd felt her stomach tighten with panic, knowing Thursday was the night Ryan went there with his friends. But the main room drew her in with its comforting smells of pizza and beer, so that even when she saw him, she walked by as if she didn't. He was at the other end of the hall by the billiards tables. He and his buddies had turned their chairs around to watch a game of pool between one of their own and a woman about twice the size of each of them, who circled the table in very re-straining jeans and with a healthy amount of attitude.

Anya carried her Cuban martini to the booth closest to the restrooms and stirred it with her pinky. From the safety of her wooden bench she glanced at Ryan and saw that his face had filled out a little, probably from eating his mother's food again. In the month they'd been apart, he'd let his beard grow into a sort of oval around his jaw. Soon he'd look like his friends, she thought, a sweatshirt pressing tight against a soft lump of stomach. She was smart to have gotten rid of him. She took a sip of her martini and let it leave its vermouthy taste on her lip. One of his friends had spotted her and was tapping Ryan's arm. It was too late to slide deeper into her booth without looking like she'd been spying. Now they were going to be moaning and negotiating whether Ryan ought to take one for the team and leave by himself, or if they'd show a united front and head out together. He was playing the good soldier now, submitting himself to the chore of getting up, hooking his thumbs through his belt loops, and looking at her dejectedly. She rolled her eyes and motioned for him to sit back down. It was fine.

She lingered over her drink until it was mostly water with an aftertaste of rum and sugar. The pool game was over; the loser was taking out twenty dollars to pay the woman with the big ass. Soon his friends were getting up to leave, and Ryan was giving them the signal to go on without him.

"Hi," he said.

"Hi."

He looked around. "Is this okay?"

"Whatever."

"You look . . ."

"Tired?"

"No. Great!"

She gave him a mistrustful look.

"You do. You want me to get you another drink, or are you gonna call the police on me?"

She slid her glass away and stood up.

"I'm kidding. I'm kidding. Sit down." He reached to grab her arm but stopped himself. "I saw you moved."

"What?"

"There was a moving van."

"You were driving around my place?"

"I just passed it, relax. Where you staying at now?"

"None of your business."

"Jesus. Look, I'm just coming by to say I'm sorry, okay? It's my fault, I man up. But it was an accident."

"Whatever."

"No. Anya. Just hear me. I'm not saying we have to be back tomorrow. I know you're doing what you gotta do. And I gotta work out my thing. But I'm just telling you I'm here."

She breathed in. "I appreciate it."

"It doesn't feel so bad, right?"

"What?"

"Us sitting here like this." After a while he said, "You want a ride home?"

She wasn't sure why she agreed. It seemed mean to decline the offer now that they'd practically signed a peace treaty. He drove slowly, as though in amends for speeding the last time, or else to drag out the short time they had together in the car. She'd guessed correctly about Ryan moving in with his mother after he'd been forced to vacate their bridal-shop apartment. It was temporary, he said. He was thinking he'd start going to school, maybe to the criminal justice college right here in the county.

"That's your new plan," she said, "to be a cop?"

"You always thought I was dumb."

"I never said that. I think you're smart."

"Smart enough to know how dumb I am, right?"

She held back from answering. Ryan always got on her nerves when he started talking this way, expecting her to applaud plans that turned out to be completely hollow. Blithering about the landscaping business he was going to start with his cousin, declaring his proposal to go to culinary school, if he happened to be watching that loud Italian chef on TV. Now he wanted to be a police officer. Bravo. Meanwhile she was still waiting tables, her own life on hold for almost two years. She didn't want to feel resentful; no doubt he was only trying to show her that he was "thinking about the future."

But a future with Ryan would be like staying in Russia. You could find a man like him on every corner in Dolsk, swearing that he intended to start a clean life as of Monday.

At the top of the hill Anya instructed Ryan to turn left. She pointed to her street of narrow Gothic houses and let him pull up to the curb. A lamp above the door bathed the old porch in dusky yellow light, but most of the windows upstairs were dark. Ryan rested his hand atop her knee in a reluctant farewell, a kindly smile narrowing his blue eyes. He had a face that could make even sadness look pleasant. She glanced up at her dark window again and unlatched her seatbelt.

"Can I come in and see your place?"

"That's not a good idea."

"Right." He patted her knee lightly in agreement and disappointment.

In the restricted space of the car she leaned in to hug him good night, smelling the aftershave-tinged sweat on his neck. And then he turned and kissed her as naturally as if he'd been given permission, the salty flavor of his mouth killing the aftertaste of stale alcohol in her own. Soon her lips were numb and her chin raw. Ryan's palm had traveled up her side, coming to a reticent stop somewhere between her breast and armpit. She reached in and fumbled with his buckle, grazing the soft hairs of his belly, suddenly and insensibly horny. Ryan was leaning his whole weight on her, while her head jammed up against the molded plastic armrest.

"Oww!"

He moved away and straightened up. "Did I hurt you?"

"No," she said, annoyed. "I'm just not comfortable."

"Let's go in."

She pushed him back onto his seat. "Whatever we're doing, we're doing in this car." She leaned down and unhitched his belt, going to work on him in an assertive manner that she imagined to be debauched but that would have been more seductive if it weren't for the sentimental way he kept trying to stroke her hair. "Come on," he urged quietly, "let's go inside."

"Fine," she said. "Wait here."

She got out of the car and mounted the front steps, unlocking the door and letting it squeak closed. She tiptoed up to her room on the second floor and found her working papers in the drawer beside her bed. They were in the same Ziploc, only a little bent and creased from when Ryan had stuck them in his glove compartment. Downstairs she made a stop in the dim kitchen and slid the bag under the ice cube trays in the freezer.

Ten minutes later he was in her room unlacing his boots while she lit a candle. He let his jeans fall and kicked them backward into a corner, and strolled around naked for a while, lifting each item on her vanity table: her library copy of Agatha Christie and her keepsake box. He examined the laminated card wedged into her mirror frame—the icon of her name saint, Anna of Kashin. He seemed to be divining facts about her life through these small articles. Anya reclined on her pillow and watched him. The room was small enough that all four walls could be seen at once in the trembling blur of the candle. So this was what their marriage had turned into, she thought, an affair to be kept in the confines of a tiny camera-box of a room.

She had dwelled on it—on that evening, on Ryan's large body in her bed—while she'd been in Erin's office, nodding at

Erin's reasonable, discouraging voice. She had let him spend that night, and the next, skipping Saturday almost by silent agreement, and meeting again Sunday. How could she explain to Erin how different it was now, to be eating oranges together on her bed, letting Ryan massage her feet—how simple the pleasures were now that she didn't need to win favor or pacify him. On their third night he'd asked her if they were going to get back together for real, meaning did she plan on lifting his restraining order. "Maybe when you're good," she'd purred, ambiguously.

The sky was pearly and dark by the time she got home from Erin's office. The oaks and maples lining her street had become black shapes shrouding porchlights and windows. Upstairs she unlocked the door to her room and found Ryan lying on her quilted bedcover with his sneakers still on his feet.

"What are you doing here, who let you in?"

He pointed at the door to the bathroom, which Anya shared with a Salvadorian couple. "Your roommates."

She had never called them that. Except for a few meekly smiling greetings, Anya had not spoken to either the girl or the guy. Tomorrow it would be someone else on that side of the wall. The place was like a bus terminal. It would be a while before she'd be able to afford something better, with what she was paying Erin.

"I called you," he said. "You didn't pick up."

"You're wearing shoes on my bed."

Ryan pried the heel of one sneaker with the toe of the other and let both shoes drop to the carpet. He slid over to one side of the bed where, on the nightstand, she noticed for the first time a bouquet of flowers. It was made up of yellow mums and orange daisies, hydrangeas, violet snapdragons, and carnations, the sort of mixed bouquet you could pick up at a supermarket, wrapped in plastic with scalloped edges.

"Happy anniversary."

"You're kidding. What is this?" She looked at the cardboard box he'd picked up off the floor and set down on the bedspread. Ryan opened up the flap and pulled out a stainless-steel appliance with a U-shaped base and a polished cranium. It looked like a small hunchbacked android.

"It's a juicer," he said.

She came closer and touched its chrome hood. Ryan lifted open the top to let her take a look at the serrated cone and gear system.

"Where'd you get it?"

"I saw it on TV and thought of you. You can squeeze oranges, lemons. You can make mojitos."

"I'm supposed to squeeze juice with this, when?"

"You said you wanted to eat natural so you didn't have to binge at the diner."

"Look at all these parts. You think I'm gonna spend a half hour taking it apart and washing it?"

"It's easy, look—"

"Where am I supposed to put it, Ryan? In the kitchen where someone's going to take it?"

"Just keep it in your room."

"And carry it downstairs?"

"Jesus, throw it away then!" He knocked the android down so it fell sideways on the bed.

"Don't get mad at *me*, Ryan! You know it's not going to make a difference. I'm not getting that order lifted!"

He looked at her with a cringing semiawareness of what

she'd just said. "I don't care what you do." The hurt and dis-
gust on his face seemed less emotional states than physical instincts.

"You can't just come over like this," she said defensively.

"I wanted to surprise you."

"Me and everybody else who saw you."

"Take a Seconal and calm down. Why are you so para-
noid? I'm the one who would get my ass ripped for this, not
you."

"What do you want, Ryan?"

"Wow. You know how to kill a special occasion."

She made a heroic effort not to roll her eyes.

"We're still married," he said.

"We gave it a shot."

"Bullshit. It's not giving it a shot when you always act like
it's gonna end."

She watched him kneel and lace up his sneakers. There
were murmurs of Spanish on the other side of the wall, in the
bathroom, and the creaking sound of a door opening and
closing in the hallway. He grabbed his jacket off the school-
house chair by her window. Already she could feel the first
clammy touch of loneliness that was going to descend on her
as soon as he was gone.

"You never thought it was real," he said without looking at
her.

Anya waited until his footsteps were at the bottom of the
stairs and closed her door. They'd managed to have a whole
fight before she'd even removed her coat. She tossed it on the
bed and sat down on the edge of her mattress, pressing her
fingers hard into her eyes. She was so tired, tired of waiting
for some big event to occur in her life, while things only
dragged on and on. In the locked bathroom, someone was

turning on the faucet. She'd have to wait to wash her hands. Soon the shower was running. She'd have to wait to pee. Everything in her life was about waiting. It was over with Ryan, she knew, though it would take time for her desire for him to pass. She'd have to overcome the urge to look for him as she had that time, like some gaunt animal migrating uphill before a flash flood without quite knowing why. She was suddenly glad that her physical exhaustion would keep her thoughts away so she could fall asleep. She heard footsteps on the unvarnished floor downstairs, the shower still running next door, but these noises seemed to come from inside her half-alive mind.

Within five months she got her permanent status papers, and almost as soon as she unfolded the letter, Anya knew she was done with all of it—with this town, with the diner, with Ryan. They receded just like that, like signs on the highway. She flew home to visit her parents in the summer, when the evenings in Dolsk stayed light, and joined her father for his therapeutic walks, returning when the sky was dimming and her mother was still weeding the flowerbeds and watering the rows of parsley and onions that grew almost to the steps of their door.

After she moved to New York City, she made a practice of optimism, taking a marketing research class at Brooklyn College and waiting tables at a steakhouse with clubby decor and a big wine list, where businessmen came to impress their clients and left her bountiful tips.

For a while Anya sometimes thought she saw him, coming out of a subway car or standing in the cavernous entrance of a bar in the East Village. But of course the city was full of men

with the same oval jaw and big stooped shoulders. She'd zero
in on one and tell herself it was him, but only to give herself
a little jolt, a little scare as if for pleasure. Once she was almost sure. She'd gotten off at Fifty-ninth Street to walk past
the Saint Patrick's Day Parade, wanting to catch the last of the
afternoon spirit before she started her evening shift. The parade had almost been spoiled by the on-and-off rain. It was
five o'clock, and the sun was coming out again. Packs of
carousers were stumbling into the side streets along Fifth Avenue, hollering drunken, nonsensical messages to one another, directions to pubs where they were planning to meet
up later. She saw him then, the side of his face first, flushed
from drinking and shouting mock insults to his friends still
at the barricades. The same light auburn hair just starting to
curl at the back of his neck, the solid body, now half-slumped
on a girl under his arm. The girl, judging by her face, was
very young but already had the low-slung behind of a woman.
She turned first, spying Anya staring, causing him to turn,
too. Except it wasn't him, but a boy with wide-set eyes and a
besotted smirk that spread as if at the knowledge of a fate he
had avoided. The beating in her chest settled to a slow, hard
thump, and her feet carried her on through the dispersing
crowd.

DEBT

ALL AFTERNOON LEV HAS WORRIED that his niece and her husband won't find his house. It is easy to miss the turnoff of Todd Road and get lost in a maze of half-paved, wooded roads that are part of the town's semirural fantasy about itself. He is relieved now to see the step-van pulling into his driveway, the late sun bouncing in a streak off the vehicle's metal siding.

"Yes, okay, I have the address," Sonya's husband told him earlier today, when Lev was giving him directions.

"The address won't help. Just listen to me . . ."

"I am *listening.*"

It had been one of those exchanges where the other person's sentences seem always to begin in the middle of your own.

Three years ago Sonya sent him and Dina a photo of herself and Meho, in a wedding chapel with vinyl records and photos of old movie stars on the walls. A year and a half later a second picture arrived in the mail: a professional snapshot of a dark-eyed infant girl posing on a cushion, a studio backdrop of painted clouds behind her. "Our angel has arrived," it said beneath. When Lev attached the card to their refrigerator, Dina had wondered out loud why someone would burden her child with a name like Andjela Bliss.

The van honks its horn in the middle of the driveway. Lev can see a thin, tanned arm wagging at him. "Take a look at our hot-truck, *dyadya Lyova!*" Sonya shouts as they brake in front of the garage. She hops out and waits for Meho to close the door on the other side. Meho removes his sunglasses and folds them into his T-shirt collar. He is older than Sonya by a good fifteen years, something Lev hadn't noticed in the photograph, shorter than Lev expected, but with a chest and arms that look like they've been built on weight machines. And yet coming up the driveway, he and Sonya share a peculiar resemblance: her hair is dyed black, as if to match Meho's, and her tan is opaque, a solarium version of his natural skin tone. She's slim to the point of gauntness, the result of some kind of exercise mania the two of them must be involved in together.

They've spent Friday and Saturday nights selling food out of their van at a music festival on Long Island, arranging to stop at Lev's house in Golden's Bridge on their way back to Baltimore. It's the first time they've driven so far north of the craft fairs, flea markets, and motorcycle rallies they usually work around the Maryland and Delaware coasts. In the summer the big money is in concerts, Sonya has told him.

"Meho, my uncle Lyova," she says, giving Lev a cheek. "The brainy side of my family. Half an hour with him is like getting a college degree." She rubs Lev's shoulder merrily.

"You're very kind, Sonechka."

"It's true, he knows everything," she says as Lev leads them inside.

"I'm just a garbage collector," he says, and laughs, bringing them out to the deck, where Dina is setting plates on the wobbly patio table.

Dina wears the loose-fitting linen dress she puts on practically every weekend during the summer, a dress without a waistline that Lev thinks resembles a smock, though Dina is convinced it looks chic in the countryish way she's come to like.

"This is a *dream*," Sonya says, gazing at the sectioned-off part of the hillside, which Dina has reclaimed as a garden. "When I was growing up, my idea of heaven was a garden like this. Did you plant it?"

Dina laughs. "Who else?"

"I bet you could teach gardening."

"Oh sure," Dina says skeptically. "Another thing I need."

It has always been hard to tell if Sonya is utterly earnest or entirely insincere in her flattery. When she was twelve, Lev can recall, coming to stay with them for the first time (her mother had put her on the Greyhound), she'd told them how happy she was to see them both again. The "again" had prompted a little laugh of disbelief from Dina; they'd left Tbilisi eleven years earlier, when Sonya was not even two. She couldn't possibly have remembered them! It had been almost taxing to watch the child laboring so hard to be lovable, awed by everything in their house and speaking in that affectedly precious tone borrowed from her mother, who had called Lev a year earlier to ask him to sign an affidavit attesting she was Emik's widow. It was 1990 and almost impossible to get a visa without family in America. She didn't want any money or

help, Alla said, only Lev's signature. At the end of the phone
call she'd been effusively grateful. He had agreed of course,
all the while wanting her to know she ought to expect nothing of him after she'd depleted and divorced his brother.
"Don't thank me," he had told her. "Thank Sonya."

Lev uncorks the Chardonnay with a little rocking motion
and pours two glasses for Sonya and Meho, then carries one
to the baluster, where Meho stands with his hands jammed in
his pockets.

"It must be an adventure to drive somewhere new every
weekend."

Meho turns to him slowly. He doesn't answer but points
his chin in the direction of the low, inflamed sunset. "Is it always like this?"

"As long as we pay the bill." Lev waits for a laugh, but the
man only nods solemnly.

Sonya has settled in beside Dina in one of the patio chairs
to show the photos she's brought. "Oh, she does have a happy
little face," Dina pipes. "And what are those?"

"Garnets. That's her birthstone."

"I see," Dina says, her way of acting innocent about things
she doesn't fully approve of. When they called to congratulate
Sonya on her baby, Dina had asked if the name was mis-
spelled in the announcement, before Sonya explained that
"Andjela" was how it was written in Croatia, where Meho was
from.

"You don't think it's a little early for that?"

"They're earrings, not a tattoo," says Sonya. "She'll want
them later anyway."

"I guess." Dina gets up to find napkins while Meho sits
down beside Sonya, laying a watchful hand on her knee. His

eyes are weighed down by heavy brows with a permanent, crescent-shaped wrinkle between them. He looks at Sonya with an expression Lev can't quite discern, a look that could be shorthand for "boredom" or "patience" or nothing at all. Lev edges his chair closer to the table, where Dina has set out a bowl of red beans in walnut sauce beside a platter of fried eggplant strips. She's carrying a cast-iron pot of pilaf when she arrives from the kitchen.

"What kind of food do you sell at your shows?" Lev asks.

"Sandwiches, cabbage rolls . . ." Sonya answers, watching Dina lift the foggy top and let out the garlic-soaked steam.

"Real food," Meho says. "But they don't know the difference. They want only chili dogs, cheese dogs, Chicago dogs. They'll eat cat litter, as long as you deep-fry it and put it on a stick."

"Plus college kids at concerts are always trying to screw you," Sonya adds, scooping spoonfuls of beans on her plate. "They'll take a bite out of a sandwich and then try to return it. I'm like 'Who do you think we are, McDonald's?' "

"People are stupid," Meho says, chewing.

"Which?" says Dina.

"People."

"In general?"

"Yes."

"Here's an example," Sonya says. "We sell meat dumplings. If someone wants a dumpling, I say, 'Two for one, or three for two?' "

Dina blinks. "Two for one or . . . ?"

"Three for two."

"But that's not a bargain," Dina says, then hesitates, pausing to think.

"You can't hold up my line to do math. Next!" Sonya shouts, as though into a crowd, laughing and spilling a little of her wine. Meho plucks a napkin off to blot it.

"I see," Dina says dryly. "Well, I guess that's one way of making money."

"I suppose you need intuition for that sort of thing," Lev adds more kindly. He is glad his own work spares him from having to form such low opinions of people. Selling, by definition, puts you in an inferior position, he thinks. To right the balance, people who sell for a living are always forming cynical and manipulative attitudes about others.

"Her talent was getting completely wasted when I met her," Meho says.

"That's how he started talking to me."

"She was working at the makeup counter in the drugstore. Every time I walked in, she was talking to another lady, or doing her face. This girl, she could sell you anything. She could sell you last year's snow. You'd be listening to her and wondering how you could have ever lived without last year's snow. But I can tell you, she was not one who ate her own bullshit," Meho says. "She just liked selling, that's all. I asked her, how much are they paying you here?"

"It was eight dollars an hour," Sonya cuts in.

"I took her out one night. I said, let's go get Chinese food in Sharpsburg—this town that was two hours away. She says okay! Imagine, you give a woman a proposition like that, let's drive two hours for Chinese food. And she says yes! You know she's not the kind of woman you're going to need to read poetry to all night."

Dina glances at Lev uncomfortably.

"We were driving back from Sharpsburg, and I said, come and work for me for *ten* dollars an hour."

"But the joke's on him," Sonya finishes. "Because now I take half!"

So this is their love story, Lev thinks. A sad one, the story of people who've fallen into each other's arms out of some shared knowledge that nobody else gave a damn about them.

The drugstore job is news to him, too. Last time Sonya visited them, four years ago, she laughed at all of Lev's jokes and told him and Dina, unconvincingly, that she was supporting herself by working as a photographer's assistant. She was tall, looked older than sixteen, but the word that had come first to mind had been *mileage*. The way she crossed her legs and leaned forward, how she didn't pause to exhale her cigarette smoke but simply let it pass out of her mouth while she spoke or laughed. It didn't seem to Lev that girls got this way by merely growing up. He hoped that she was indeed working as a photographer's assistant. A year before that Sonya's mother had called Lev demanding to know if Sonya was staying with them. She wasn't. But a week later Lev received a call from Sonya, who was asking to borrow money. She wouldn't say where she was living. When Lev had requested some phone coordinates, she'd given him only the number of her pager. He had Western Unioned her $200 the next day, dialed the long sequence of digits, and reached an enervating tone, like the bug-crushing sound of a fax machine. When Sonya called him back a few days later, neither of them spoke about the money. After that he wired her $300 every couple of months or so. He didn't want her doing God-knows-what for a few bucks. And wasn't it to his credit in some way, he thinks now, that she's managed to avoid a worse turn in life?

Lev can feel the air tickling the hair on the back of his neck. It has gotten cool suddenly. There is only an isolated bright spot now above some woods where the sun has set. "Maybe we should get these young people some sweaters," he suggests.

"And some real drinks," says Dina. "Meho hasn't seen the bar yet. Have you?"

Lev watches his footing down the dim, carpeted stairwell. The basement tour has become something of a routine in their house, and now he and Dina almost never set out the serious alcohol beforehand, so that Lev can take the guests down to "the bar," built by the previous owners, who once carpeted the basement and turned it into what must have been their idea of a leisure room. The leather sofa is scratched with claw marks and scarred by cigarette burns, the plywood paneling redolent with stale cigar odor. Behind the actual bar Lev keeps only five or six bottles at a time. When he and Dina first moved in ten years ago, their son already away studying piano at Juilliard, Lev had hoped to restock the bar properly, if only out of a vague sense of debt to its purpose. But over the years he'd found another use for it, and now when visitors follow him downstairs, what they see, along the lit-up shelves that once gave a showcase treatment to shakers and highball glasses, are rows of framed patent certificates. They fill the whole back wall, so that guests are often forced into a silent count with their eyes, just as Meho pauses to do.

Lev snaps the track lighting to make the patents easier to see and goes to inspect the few bottles lined up along the back well. In the halogen lamplight he finds the silver tray with its six engraved mini-cups, part of the after-dinner ritual, a wedding gift to his parents fifty years ago.

"Your awards?" Meho says. He's seated himself on a

leather stool and folds his elbows on the bartop as though he were in a real pub waiting to be served.

"They're *ideas*," Lev corrects. "Hennessey or Rémy Martin?"

Meho points at the black bottle, then squints at a certificate above Lev's head. "A nice frame," he says professionally.

"That one is very special. It is a design for a filter—not a filter, really a magnet—that goes inside a helicopter turbine." Lev sets the Rémy down to mime the mechanics with his hands. "If a helicopter lands in a desert and raises a cloud of sand, this charges the tiny dust so it doesn't get inside and dull the motor."

Meho watches him with an expression of bland amusement provoked more by the naked eagerness on Lev's face than by what he is actually saying.

"These six," Lev points to the yellowed patents on the brick wall, "I brought with me. But all the others I received here in America." He knows he is carrying on, almost against his better judgment. It is unusual for him to wax on for so long about himself. Most of the time his guests are deferential, or well bred enough to barrage him with questions about the certificates, or else to convey their esteem silently. He does not want Meho to mistake his enthusiasm for bragging. Though perhaps this enthusiasm, he fears now, is only a way of bragging without seeming to. "Well, it isn't as many patents as your Tesla," he finishes finally.

"What?" Meho says, tightening his brows.

"Nikola Tesla. The father of coil transistors, fluorescent lights, radio—"

"Yes, I know who Tesla is."

"A fellow Croatian."

"He was from Croatia, a Serb." Meho's eyes are already fixed on something else, a framed photo of Sasha in a bow tie, posing with a high-foreheaded man in a tuxedo. "Your son?"

"That's him with George Rothman, who conducts the Riverside Symphony. At Alice Tully Hall." He can hear how it sounds suddenly: meaningless explanation, names and places that seem all the more hollow for their intimations of greatness. But when Meho glances at the patent for the helicopter magnet again, Lev can't help himself. "We got a contract from Defense to develop it."

"The army?" Meho says, his eyes more alert.

"The air force. Five hundred thousand in grants."

"They gave *you* five hundred thousand?" Meho says, looking around the basement, as if its sorry state casts doubt on this fact.

"Not in my *pocket.* So the company can develop the idea."

"So why do you not work for yourself? You like for others to make money on your ideas?"

It is as if some bird of meaning has escaped the cage. Perhaps he's explained something poorly, Lev thinks. Unless this man makes a habit of misunderstanding things deliberately. "It's how research works," he says. "A lottery. It's all risk."

"Yes, I understand risk. But you are worried *now*?" Meho grips the bottle and gazes around the fluorescent-lit basement. "You have what, seventeen, eighteen here?"

The number is twenty-four, but Lev doesn't trouble to correct him. He takes the tray of cups and follows Meho up the steps.

Outside there is still some daylight left in the sky, but the trees have turned black, blurring with the darkness that's started to encroach on the lawn. The deck and gray siding look pewter in the bluish cast of evening. The women sit with cardigans draped around their shoulders. Lev reaches between them and sets the tray on the glass tabletop. He's learned just recently, from an American guest, that it's in fact a set of mini kiddush cups, intended for Sabbath wine, not liquor. He wonders if his parents knew this, keeping them on display all those years? He pours the cognac around, too old to unlearn his ignorance now, he tells himself, and tosses down his drink. It warms him instantly.

"We had these!" Sonya says, picking up one of the cups and turning it in her fingers. She strains to examine the engravings, which are fine like the engravings of old stamps. "Maybe ours were darker," she says, and takes a sip off the rim.

It's the same set; after his parents died, the cups had gone to Emik, who'd let the silver tarnish. Years later, when Emik decided to visit New York, Lev had asked him to bring them, wanting to have some keepsake from his parents. The morning he'd picked up his brother at JFK, Emik didn't neglect to mention how empty the apartment would feel without them. That he had inherited everything else, including the apartment itself, seemed to Lev an ungenerous point to make.

"Help yourself," Lev says, refilling Meho's already empty glass, while Dina turns to Sonya.

"Who do you leave the baby with when you travel?"

"There's a woman in the neighborhood who takes her," says Sonya. "Her husband's dead, she lives alone. It's a good arrangement. She says she likes it when there's another little soul in the room."

Meho startles them with a deep, oddly charming laugh. "Let me tell you about this lady," he says. "She sits in a chair

all day long doing her needlepoint and channel-flipping."
He makes a deprecating gesture with his thumb.

"And who else is going to take a kid for a whole weekend?"
Sonya says.

"Doesn't your mother live close by?" asks Dina, her curiosity at work again. It's always best to let her ask her questions without interrupting, Lev has learned, since she will
otherwise turn her inquisitiveness on him and ask why *he* is so
uncomfortable.

"I'm not about to start asking her for favors," says Sonya.
"She's busy with her own life."

"Doesn't she want to see her granddaughter?"

"She can see Andjela whenever she decides to visit us. I'm
not stepping foot in her house as long as that monkey's
there."

Lev snorts a laugh. Sonya has captured Alla's husband
perfectly—the long space between Sergey's nose and mouth
that has always given his face a simian quality. Alla used to
hang around him even when they were all students, Lev
remembers. At the Polytech where they'd studied, she'd ignored Emik cruelly. Not until she was twenty-eight—and not
so young by those times—did she give him a second look. But
weeks before they'd gone to the ZAGS to register their marriage, Lev had seen her in a café, sitting across from Sergey,
while he fed her a square of cake. It had been a mistake to tell
Emik. Lev had only brought more rage down on himself. As
for their parents, they'd been useless, glad someone would
have him—their biggest fear was that Emik was going to end
up alone because of his "infirmity." *"What woman with a healthy
head is going to crawl into a sickbed?"* had been their mother's favorite remark back then.

Years later, on their ride to Niagara Falls, Emik had told
Lev that he didn't blame Alla for their rotting marriage or
her infidelity, which she no longer bothered to conceal. He
didn't blame her, he had said, nodding off in the passenger
seat on their way to yet another imperative American land-
mark. He'd struggled to stay awake all that week, taking naps
on Lev's couch, or in the jacked front seat of the car when
they stopped at filling stations. His problems with Alla were
the natural consequences of his bad luck—the bad luck of
having become "meager as a man," as he put it. If only his di-
abetes had made him go blind instead of limp, he joked.

"She doesn't tell anybody she's a grandmother," Sonya
says. "She's trying to get pregnant, actually."

"Isn't she almost *fifty*?" Dina's voice is thick with interest.

"Yeah, well. No rest for the devil."

Lev pours a second shot for Meho and refills his own
glass. The cognac tastes acidy, but in another moment the
warmth spreads to his loins and he's able to recapture the
glaring, misted light of Niagara, where Emik, pale and
ragged, asked if it was possible for him not to leave, to stay in
the United States with Lev. They would need to hire a lawyer,
Lev explained, surprised by this turn in the conversation.
Even if they built a case for asylum, what would he do here?
he asked Emik. He was too weak to tackle the job of starting a
new life—he himself had acknowledged that much. Emik said
he hadn't really thought it through. And then the days passed
without either of them bringing it up again.

Lev tosses back another ounce of Rémy Martin to rinse
out the sourness in his mouth. A refill for Meho, to be com-
panionable.

"For two years I slept on a tiny mattress we got from some

charity," Sonya continues. "I asked my mother to buy me a normal-sized bed, and she acted like I was asking for a boat. And the day *he* moved in, she went out and bought the two of them a king-sized Sealy to have fun on."

"So then you got her old mattress," Meho cuts in. "Problem solved. How long are you going to cry about this?"

For a second Lev feels almost warmhearted toward him.

"I'm just saying," Sonya answers, "that she's got a lot to apologize for."

There are already smears on the cups, salty oils from fingers that Lev will have to wipe off tonight. Tarnishes are hard to get rid of if you don't clean them right away; the abrasives he used after Emik had flown back to Tbilisi had left the engravings dull in spots.

And then, not three months later, Emik was dead. He had died in the same apartment they'd grown up in, among the old furniture and crystal, among the dense stacks of magazines their father had never thrown out—issues of *Science and Life, Novy Mir,* whose pages were warped and stuck together after years of going unread. Whenever Lev had imagined that day, he thought of the wide balcony, half shaded by branches from a walnut tree. From the courtyard came the scudding sounds of kids herding a soccer ball around; he envisioned Emik falling asleep on the couch beside the balcony doors to the soft noises below and never waking up.

For years afterward he would hear of some ignoramus or another referring to Emik's death as a suicide. An old classmate, a former colleague, alluding in an offhand way to an overdose of insulin. No one said it to his face, but word always got back. And the progress of time, instead of dispelling these speculations, only hardened them.

"Oww!" Sonya slaps her ankle. It has gotten dark now, a

darkness bearing mosquitoes. Lev tears a paper match from the matchbook on the table and shelters it in his palm, igniting the citronella candle. A scent like lemon and car wax fills the air, and Sonya's face swims back into light. "When Sergey moved in," she says, scratching the bite, "I just told myself, Keep your mouth shut and bide your time." It's apparent that she's been chronicling all this for years. She looks determined, in the candle glow, to straighten out some record.

"Please eat," Dina says.

Sonya pokes around the muddle of her pilaf and beans. Everyone else's plate is empty. For a moment it is quiet, possible to hear the medley of chirping insects and the deeper, steady croakings of frogs.

"You live in a nice place," Meho says.

"We like it," Dina answers.

"We live above a freeway," Sonya adds, apropos of nothing.

"We liked it here, so we stayed," Dina says.

Lev edges his chair in closer for an explanation. "We were sponsored by a temple in this area."

Dina glances at him warily. He has a habit of sharing things she prefers to leave out, though it's something he's rarely aware of until after the unnecessary detail has been disclosed.

"What does this mean, *sponsored*?" Meho says.

"They helped us with little things," Dina answers. "English classes, they gave us some used clothes to wear to job interviews . . ." In her voice there is almost a lazy reluctance about the topic itself.

"And jobs also, they helped you find jobs?"

They had, in fact. One of the members of the temple was a manager in a company that had hired Lev on a contract basis.

"Finding work was not the hard part. Lev had many pub-
lications."

"You go to this temple?" Meho asks, turning to Lev.

"No. We don't," Dina answers. "Not anymore. It
wasn't . . . for us." But then, rethinking, she adds, "Sometimes we go on holidays, and we make contributions." She
smiles serenely, as if to say their debts have been settled.

"My first year I found only two kinds of work," Meho tells
Lev. "Carrying crates off a truck *to* a store, and carrying crates
from a store to the truck. My concessions business took me six
years to start."

Lev nods sympathetically. "And now you see how well it's
doing."

"As well as it's going to do. We cannot work more than two
shows a weekend. Maybe three, but that's all."

"It's not the kind of business that can *grow*," Sonya says.
"And all this driving around with a child. What we really want
is to open a place of our own."

It's starting to dawn on Lev why they might have driven so
far out of their way now.

"You're talking about a restaurant?"

"Just Soups. That's what we want to call it," Sonya says,
giggling. "We'll add other things to the menu later."

"You already have a menu?"

"We're ready to open it tomorrow if we had the funds.
We've found a place, but . . ."

Meho is staring down into his plate, letting Sonya take
over.

"We've saved up fifteen thousand, but the banks won't
give us more. We've gone to *two*, and it's always the same
thing . . . we can't get a second mortgage because we don't

own a house. We'd have to grow the business we have now, and start taking on debt and paying it off to show we're responsible. But that's impossible because, like he said, we can't work *more* than we already do."

Dina has joined Lev in his benign silence. It seems almost impossible to continue this discussion without raising the question of how much they need.

"Life," Lev says wistfully. "We can't work more, and we can't work less." It makes him sound dim, he realizes, or possibly cruel. But he knows he needs to discuss this question with Dina in private. She might agree to offer a sum—not huge but not insulting.

Meho is squinting off into space with the inward look of someone trying to maintain his dignity. Lev guesses it was Sonya's idea to ask for money, that her husband has gone along with it in spite of his faint contempt for such solicitations. Though of course it may be just the opposite.

The frogs fill the silence with their croaking. Meho and Sonya are quiet, waiting for Lev to say something more, and when he doesn't, Sonya takes a deep breath, savoring the air dramatically. "It must be nice to sit out here every evening," she says.

"Last summer this was all a pile of wood," Lev answers, glad the other conversation has been aborted. "The deck kept us busy for months. Every weekend we were making trips down to the Home Depot." On his lips it sounds as though he's done the work himself. Though there is some truth in that, since the carpenter they hired dawdled, and he and Dina *did* finish the banister themselves, and the paint job.

"I went to the Home Depot last month," Meho says. "And the salesman told me I could get a line of credit, no questions, for thirty thousand dollars unsecured. I thought, Are they crazy? Two American banks turn me down, and these people want to give me money for nothing? Then I understood, if I buy from them, they want me to borrow from them, so *they* can control my money instead of the American banks."

"The *American* banks?" Dina laughs. "And what is Home Depot?"

"They're Jewish."

For a moment Dina's lips are stalled in confusion. When she speaks, it comes out like a childish protest. "But they don't take your money, they *give* it to you."

"Correct. But I'm talking about control. Having money is one thing, having control of it is different." The patience in his voice suggests he is stating something apparent. And for a moment Lev can't tell where the problem in the reasoning lies, aside from it leading to one illegitimate conclusion.

"So the banks don't want to control the money?" Dina says.

"You are misunderstanding me." Meho grins knowingly at her glassy smile, to show that he can see what's coming his way if he takes her bait. "Say something about one, they think you are talking about all." He isn't addressing Dina anymore, so much as withdrawing into a private conference with himself. Sonya has fixed her eyes on the glow of the candle, her fingers splayed on the tabletop. Her hand resembles a sea creature fastening itself to the floor of the ocean, making itself invisible until a danger passes.

"You look tired, my dear," Lev says, getting up out of his chair. Sonya raises her eyes at him, startled and then relieved. "I'll show you both to your room," Lev tells them. And one by one they begin to get up, stacking the dishes and

collecting glasses marked with the dregs of wine, managing
through an awkward ceremony of thank-yous and praise of
dinner, until Lev follows them up to the second floor. He
shows them the towels in the linen closet, and the bathroom,
where he twists the shower faucet to demonstrate how to
change the temperature, while they nod at his earnest, unnecessary instructions, his final, bedtime effort to restore
peace.

"I don't care about him," Dina says when Lev is downstairs again. She runs the tap and shakes the water from her
hands. "Now we know what's in his head. But what's in *hers*?"

"What was she supposed to say?"

"Something!"

They can hear a soft shuffling of feet upstairs. Dina's
voice falls to a harsh whisper. "She didn't peep a word."

"You know she's better off with him."

Dina fiddles helplessly with the dish tray. He reaches for
her arm, draws her in. She resists at first but lets him pull
back the hair from her moist forehead with his palm. She
smells of light perspiration and cooking oil, the Green Tea
perfume she's worn for as long as he can remember. How
much easier, he thinks, when it's just the two of them, a balance that others only disturb. Without embracing her too
tightly, he holds her face and kisses it.

He tells Dina he'll put away the food, and stays in the
kitchen after she goes upstairs. In the refrigerator the shelves
are crammed with bottles of condiments they rarely use,
white Chinese takeout boxes from work that he has to move
around to make room for the leftovers. After Emik's death,
he recalls, his brother's refrigerator had been found full of
food: fruit and yogurt fresh from the market, an unopened
bottle of milk, and a stick of salami still wrapped in its brown

paper. Lev was told all this by the wife of a neighbor who had discovered Emik on the couch; the wife had been kind enough to clean the apartment before the funeral. She'd told him he hadn't been lying there very long, only a day or two. It hadn't comforted him then, but later it had. What person intending to end his life would restock his refrigerator for the weeks ahead? he'd ask himself whenever he'd hear one of the festering rumors.

There are footsteps descending the stairs, too soft and childlike to be Dina's. When he turns, he sees Sonya standing in the kitchen entryway in her jeans and an oversize T-shirt she's changed into, a face printed on it, probably of a musician from one of the shows she's worked.

"Everyone comfortable upstairs?"

"Mm." She smiles in a courteous, distant way.

"Do you need another blanket?"

She shakes her head. She doesn't seem to be in any hurry to talk about what it is she's come for. Her eyes wander around the maple cabinets, pausing on the baby picture tacked to the refrigerator.

"It's hard to leave her every week," she says. "I don't want you to think we would be asking for a donation. We only need fifteen thousand, even less—ten, as an investment, and we'd start making it back immediately."

He closes his eyes in the hope that she'll stop. "I'm not a businessman, Sonya," he says opening his eyes and looking up at her. "And I'm not . . ." He tries to clear the gravel from his voice. "I'm not a lender."

Her arms are folded tightly across her chest. She seems to be nodding, or just pondering something, a quietly miserable look on her face.

"You know I'd always help," he hears himself say, "if it concerns you or Andjela."

She doesn't look at him and continues to rub the goose bumps on her flesh.

"You're cold?" he asks.

Sonya shakes her head. He gets up anyway and finds one of Dina's cardigans on a fan-back chair, brings it to Sonya, and spreads it over her shoulders. She manages a dutiful smile, allows him to draw her into a hug. But he can feel the change—Sonya's back stiff under his arms, almost like a physical reproach. He presses her tighter until her body relaxes a little. When he lets her go, there is a wet film over her dark eyes. "I'll go up to bed now," she says.

"Okay." He smooths the sweater over her shoulders.

She turns and heads back up the stairs, and he can hear her shuffling footsteps, the sound of the door closing. When she's gone, he is glad to be alone. Even while he was holding her, it had felt like a preemptory move, putting her in a spot where she would be the one looking for an exit.

The porch lamp is still on. It draws bugs to the netted screen on the door. He finds the switch, killing the illumination on the scattered arrangement of patio chairs outside, and makes his way up to the bedroom. From now on, he thinks, she will speak his name in the same uncharitable way that she talks about all the others who've failed her.

Dina is already snoozing, asleep with the reading lamp casting a prism of light on a paperback, which lies on her chest, her reading glasses tucked between its pages. There will be no more requests, he thinks, from Sonya. No more concerts on Long Island to justify the long drive north to see them. In the morning, while the light is still gray, he'll probably be awakened by the rustle of them carrying their bags downstairs. When they leave, he hopes Dina will still be asleep. He doesn't know if he'll go downstairs or just lie and listen for the slap of the car doors, the rasp of the engine receding into a relieving silence.

THE REPATRIATES

THE LAST DAYS of Grisha and Lera Arsenyev's marriage might have been a story fashioned out of commonplace warnings. Retold, it became no longer about the Arsenyevs at all, but about the ambushes that befall the most gleefully naïve of us, still laboring under illusions. The Arsenyevs were a different sort of immigrant from those who'd washed up with the tides of asylum-seekers in the seventies and eighties. In 1994 Grisha Arsenyev's visa had been processed not by the staffs of refugee committees but by a covey of lawyers working for Hewlett-Packard, assigned to skim the cream of eastern brainpower. After his indentured servitude at HP—which lasted the five years it took the company to come through with the promised green card—Arsenyev quit and promptly got himself hired for twice as much as a quant at Morgan Stanley, building market models for mortgage traders. Whatever envy his fast climb had stirred in the hearts of others, to hear

Grisha Arsenyev talk one might guess that immigration had turned out to be the great anticlimax of his life. At the get-togethers they attended, Lera would often see her husband off in a corner, rattling his drink and talking with someone about the morbid state of American culture, the absence of any real *spirituality* here. It was known to happen to such late arrivants—the ones who'd risked nothing, forsaken little, and had not even been required by the Russian government to annul their red passports. Once, in somebody's kitchen, Lera had heard a man refer to her husband as "Lenin in Exile" and had recognized the allusion to Grisha's beard and his huge forehead heightened by baldness, and to the provokable mind that liked to assign every problem its proper place in a political chain of events. The enthusiasm with which Grisha spoke of the "opportunities" in Russia would begin to remind his listener of the sort of miscalculation made by those who marry for money and invariably realize they didn't marry for enough. In the economic upheavals he had avoided, his old colleagues who'd stayed in Moscow had started making serious money, while he was still shackled to a salary on Wall Street, of all places. So it surprised only a few when Grisha started traveling back, seeing old friends and making new ones, looking for his own golden formula. And when one of his usual weeklong trips stretched out to two months, Lera found her husband's absence something to be endured.

On the phone he told her he had no plans to return to Morgan Stanley, where he had been disregarded, he said, passed over for men whose only qualifications beyond his were that they could quote *Star Wars* and recall Yankee's scores from the Nixon era. He no longer wished to be tyrannized by bogus performance evaluations where he'd been called "judgmental" and told that he "imposed his opinion on others," before being asked to sign that shit like a forced confession. Fate, he said, had chosen a better path for him in his homeland. He was staying in Moscow to look for financiers for a business idea that would do on the Russian market what mortgage traders had done on Wall Street since the eighties: pool and repackage cheap loans for investors in one massive turbine of debt and capital. He'd build not only wealth for himself but a better life for the doctors and schoolteachers in deaf provinces, still living in run-down, vermin-infested apartments and dreaming of raising their kids in solid houses, if only Russia would grow a robust mortgage industry.

Within three months Lera had sold their Dobbs Ferry house with a view of the Hudson. *Dekabristka*, her daughter called her, joking that her devotion was like that of the Decembrist wives who followed their men to Siberia after their uprising against the monarchy. She wasn't sure if Masha meant this kindly, but when the first clouds appeared through the airplane's windows, Lera pretended they were vales of snow she was crossing by sleigh and carriage. She'd be too far away now to send Masha packages at college—scented soaps and soup mixes, magazine clippings and dried flowers from her garden. The garden itself would probably go neglected by the house's new owners, a busy professional couple with infant twins who wouldn't necessarily appreciate that Lera had spent several seasons selecting plants for full and partial shade, dragging limestone from a quarry, digging a hole for the dogwood tree to replace the diseased elm that the town had cut down. Then again, none of that mattered much now. It was Grisha who needed her, not a garden.

There was only an effete, uneven applause in the cabin

when the plane touched down on the runway in Shereme-
tyevo. At the gate Lera looked for Grisha among the people
holding bouquets and spied his head. His hair had gone the
color of a battleship a while ago, but his skin still had the
dairy-fed ruddiness of a country boy's.

"Couldn't leave anything behind," he said, smiling at her
suitcases. He slid an arm around her shoulder and nestled
her in for a quick kiss before leading her out into Moscow's
pale November evening.

Through the vibrating raindrops on the car window, she
could see the jagged monument marking the limit of the
German advance in '41 and, just beyond it, the cobalt blue of
an IKEA superstore. Billboards for cell phone companies
stood out against the soupy weather.

"I wish you would convince Masha to fly here for New
Year's," Lera said. "She says she's going to stay in the dorms
all winter."

"If she wants to stay, it's her business. She needs a ticket,
I'll send her money."

Her husband and her daughter were exactly alike. Both
liked to take a misanthropic posture, but against what, Lera
could never guess. "I just want to make plans, Grisha. So
everything isn't done at the last minute. If we're going to
start renovating, Masha won't have a place to sleep. You said
it took Olya and Kirill eight months to redo their apartment."

"Kirill wanted all his closets wired. So when he opens the
doors, they light up like refrigerators," Grisha said. "I'm a
simple man."

Grisha's cousin had been eking out a living fixing furniture when they'd left. The fact that since that time he had

made a windfall buying and selling upholstery hadn't changed Grisha's view that Kirill was fundamentally an idiot.

"You didn't forget the suit?" Grisha asked. "I'm going to Tver next week."

"It's still in its plastic. I don't know why you need an Armani jacket to talk to a bunch of bureaucrats." She had gone into the city to buy it for him before she left because he insisted it was twice as expensive on Tverskaya.

"They aren't bureaucrats. There are going to be people from SberBank, AIGK. And Stanislav Mitin, too."

On the phone Grisha had told her about Mitin, the real estate developer who'd offered to guarantee the first issue of loans, to put aside his own money if a housing market in some province collapsed. She didn't think she liked the sound of Mitin; his interest in Grisha's proposed company seemed predicated not on its profit potential but on his sharing Grisha's somewhat sanctimonious vision of a glorious and holy Russia. He'd had an Orthodox priest bless each of his newly opened businesses, Grisha had told her, which made her think the man had more than enough to atone for.

"Should I tell you about my flight?" she asked. "They sat me next to one of those Russian candy bars in pink sweatpants. She tapped my shoulder whenever she had to get up and pee. No 'excuse me.' No 'thank you.' *Tap tap.* The stewardess told her to put away her giant white leather bag, and she pointed to my purse and said, 'What about *her*? Why don't you tell her to put *hers* away?' "

"What bluebloods we have these days."

"Her husband had a tattoo on one of his fingers."

"What was it?"

"A spade. I don't know. Maybe he wasn't even her husband."

A silver chain glinted from under Grisha's collar. Lera reached over and fished it out with her nail. "What's this?" She rubbed her thumb over the small cross. Grisha gave her a dark look, like that of a teenager whose privacy has been intruded on. "It was my mother's."

She let the cross drop and reclined in her seat. In what drawer, she wondered, between what set of ironed sheets, would Grisha's dead mother, with her Komsomol and Party allegiances, have kept this silver cross?

Along the main drag of Bolshaya Cherkizovskaya, the trees had lost their leaves, revealing spare playgrounds—wooden seesaws and painted steel climbing bars between the buildings. Soon they were turning on to their old block of Khrushchev-era low-rises just past the Preobrazhenskoye metro, a neighborhood of durable, identical blocks where they'd spent the first years of their marriage.

Little had changed inside. The living room had the same massive lacquered wall unit and textured wallpaper, damaged now by pencil scrawlings of tenants' children, the same double curtains of polyester lace and cretonne. Year after year they had intended to sell the place, first waiting for the market to pick up, then worrying about dishonest agents. Finally Grisha had simply left it empty for his travels. She could see he hadn't done anything to the place, that he had probably been waiting for her to arrive and start renovating.

The next morning Lera made phone calls. She called her aunt in Krasnodar, promising to visit before New Year's, and her old friend Lidochka, who cried from joy that Lera was only three metro stops away. She called Olya, Grisha's cousin's wife, who was rushing off to Mamontovka, where she and Kirill were building a "kottedzh." Olya apologized that she couldn't stay on the phone longer, explaining that she needed to get to the suburbs before her work crew took their eighty-proof eye-opener.

A few days later Lera called in her own crew to replace the windows in the apartment. The two men who showed up asked if they could change into their work clothes in the living room. They were still in their underwear when she returned ten minutes later with a plate of cheese and glasses of juice. "We'll forgive you this time," one of them said, smiling crudely when she looked at his work boots and bare chest. The other one sniffed the juice and said, "Anything a little stronger, madam?"

"My husband wants the windowsills replaced as well," she said, leading them through the rooms. "And please take away the old glass when you're done. I don't want to give my husband more work to do." The words *my husband* were like an incantation, filling the rooms with Grisha's spirit, a Grisha who defended his wife's honor and did not tolerate grown men stripping in his home. The husband she invoked was master of his domain, a more solid presence than the one who actually lived here. The one who lived here left early and came home late, just as he'd done in Dobbs Ferry. In the mornings now he took the metro to his office in Kitai-Gorod; not quite an office, but the corner of a floor he rented from a computer company. A real office would come later, he told Lera, when he found investors for his securities firm. He was going to Tver in a few days to pitch his idea to some forward-thinking local mini-garchs. At night he stayed up working late at the computer desk in the bedroom, before

getting into bed and reading a few pages from the hardcover
on his nightstand.

"Who is that?" Lera asked one night, looking at the bull-
dog-like face on the jacket.

"Pavel Ryabushinsky." Grisha had his chin tucked into his
chest as he read.

She wedged her pelvis against the side of his hip. "A
writer?"

"He was an industrialist at the turn of the century."

"Like Rockefeller?" she said. Her fingers played with the
hair on his stomach. The warm world below the blanket had
its own rules.

Grisha didn't answer. He turned another page. Traffic
sounds floated in through the casement window. "Rockefeller
was like him," he said, nearly a minute later. "Russia was more
industrialized than America back then. The ruble was more
stable than the dollar." She felt Grisha's soft belly tighten under her stroking hand. She didn't remember when they had
developed this pattern of him not responding to her until the
last possible moment. Seductively she traced her finger along
the elastic band of his shorts. He hadn't made love to her since
she'd arrived. Now he removed her hand, patted it, and placed
it beside him on the sheet. "I have to wake up early," he said,
shutting the book and curling toward the wall.

She tried not to feel insulted. He was tired and spent by his
work. She was here now, to take care of him. She would make
Grisha a special dinner before he went on his overnight trip to
Tver on Thursday. The next morning she walked to the Preo-
brazhensky market to get groceries and fresh fish, following
the crowds rolling their handcarts down a footpath lined with
pensioners—women holding up hand-knit shawls and strings
of dried mushrooms. A battery of grandmothers stood along

the chain-link fence peddling old shoes they'd set out on newspapers. Books, dull knives, outmoded cameras, useless things. How conspicuous the elderly were here, she thought, how openly old.

She made her way through the acre of stone counters piled with carrots and potatoes, tubs of sour cabbage. Sharp gusts of wind burned her cheeks. At a table covered with egg cartons, a frizzy-haired blonde in fingerless gloves rubbed her hands together and lit up a cigarette.

"Right out of the henhouse," Lera said, and grinned. She pointed to the largest of the eggs, which had a downy feather stuck to it. "How much?"

The woman exhaled smoke through the side of her mouth. "You can't read?" She glanced down just enough for Lera to notice the prices taped to the edge of the table, then turned away to suck on her cigarette.

Lera picked up a Styrofoam container and started to load the eggs.

"Take a look at *her*," the woman said. "Self-service."

"I didn't think you could be bothered."

The blonde shook her head. "Give me that," she said, grabbing the egg carton. "At this speed you'll take all day. Can't you see you're driving away my customers?"

"Excuse me?"

"Excuse me. Excuse me," the woman said, loading eggs.

"Don't be a dandelion," Grisha told her when she complained to him in the evening. "You like to let everything raise your blood pressure." He'd finished the mushroom soup she had cooked for him and was cutting into the trout she'd served.

"You know how these people live," he said, washing down

the fish with white wine. "This egg lady probably has to get up before the roosters, use an outhouse, drive here from some *huyevo-tutuyevo*. Okay, so she has lightbulbs, thanks to Lenin's faith in electricity. You want her to tell you to have a nice day?"

"And they're all waiting for you to make their lives better," she said, finishing her wine.

He let her remark pass, apparently deeming it too foolish to argue with. "Someone looks at you wrong, Lera, and you need a sedative. What do you think I have to put up with? The last time I gave this talk that I'm giving tomorrow, some VIP picked his nose through my entire presentation. And not just digging, I mean doing an investigation."

"I don't want to argue," she said. "I only wanted to tell you about my day."

She got up and set her dishes in the small sink. She would need to look for a job here, to channel her mind toward something more purposeful than complaining. For the past two years, since the drug laboratory where she'd worked had closed its Westchester location, she had manned the reception desk at her gym three days a week. She'd taken her exit package from the lab, learned to garden, started reading novels again. She missed the gym now, missed the women telling her about the nannies they hired or the ones they'd fired because they'd discovered them stealing money or seen photographs of nephews in Hungary playing with toys that had disappeared from the house. She missed being told in confidence about the cycling instructor who'd remarried his first wife right after divorcing his third. At the gym people involved her in the theater of their daily lives as though she were a bartender handing them not towels but glasses of gin. In the evenings, when she'd tried to interest Grisha in these stories, he'd listen with a face of painful submission. When she was with him the life that gave her pleasure seemed frivolous; it was like describing a sitcom—the plots unraveled, the jokes were no longer funny. Grisha would listen until he had finished eating and then go upstairs to start his graveyard shift, working late into the night on articles about "social mortgages" and "securitization" that he submitted to Russian economic journals.

She watched him consume his dinner now, get through the trout bite by bite, gulp down his wine. His pale blue eyes looked watery from exhaustion, the skin of his nose polished as if by a sunburn. His sideburns were cut shorter in preparation for the presentation of his idea for a private loan-backing firm, a Russian Fannie Mae, as he called it. She knew she would be too frightened to start all over, the way he was doing at forty-six.

"You'll do fine," she said. "You'll see."

He smirked, though not meanly this time. Lera sat down and slid her hand across the table, touching his arm. She wanted to be a supportive wife, to do whatever fate required, though at times it seemed the most she could do was not interfere.

She went to meet her friend Lidochka in the afternoon, after Grisha boarded his train. Her friend had been going by Lidochka, not Lida, all her life, or as long as Lera remembered, a little girl's name that had followed her into her forties because of her gentleness and a reputation for being short on common sense. She covered her mouth when she saw Lera on the platform of the Ohotny Ryad metro. "Oh, my soul!" she

said, embracing her. Lidochka had once looked like a fairy,
but now her small features puckered out of a face that had
swollen and become as puffy as a flaky pastry.

They went to a café on the first floor of the Tchaikovsky
Conservatory, unadorned and nearly empty but for a few
students, which was what Lidochka must have liked about it,
Lera thought, living as she did with almost no privacy. When
Lera carried éclairs and coffee to their table, she saw tears in
Lidochka's eyes. "How I've waited for you," Lidochka said,
touching Lera's thin jacket lovingly. "Don't spend your
money. I'll have Natasha pick you up a good coat on her next
trip." She looked out through the window at the dry, tiny
snowflakes and added, "It's going to be a bad winter for or-
phans." Natasha, her daughter, traveled to China every few
months, buying up merchandise that she and her new lover,
whom she'd moved in with, sold around to the kiosks. Meanwhile Natasha's five-year-old son and husband still lived with
Lidochka in the two-room apartment, a domestic situation
that was now in its second year.

"He's like a son to me," she said of her son-in-law. "It
breaks my heart to watch him on the couch in the evenings,
changing the channels without saying a word. Sometimes
he goes days without speaking. Every morning I wake up and
think I'm going crazy. Then I fold my cot in the kitchen, get
a grip on myself, and tell my son-in-law to eat breakfast."

"How do you stay afloat?" Lera said.

"Oh, my dear, I still have my students. At a time like this,
though, I wish I tutored English instead of French."

"I forgot! Tell me about your trip to Paris this summer."
She wished to switch to a less desperate topic. It was clear that
Lidochka, after eleven years, could not be bothered with
small talk. To her, friendship still meant coming face-to-

face with another's unmediated existence. It was exhilarating, Lera thought, but also exhausting.

"What is there to say, they put us up in some dirty hotel outside the city. We rode into Paris in the mornings and had to stand in line on the bus for hot water. And we weren't fed; I had to carry around tins of sardines in my purse." She wiped a tear from the corner of her eye with a napkin. "I didn't want to tell you before, but now I will: I answered a classified ad in the paper for a receptionist job at a travel agency. You don't know how hard it is to find work after forty. These ads are all the same, they ask for twenty-year-olds 'without complexes.' But this one seemed reasonable. I told them I'd been a French teacher, they hired me right away. They said the bus tour was a requirement for the job, so I'd be able to tell the clients about the trips the agency sold. I'd be reimbursed as soon as I started working. But when I got back, it turned out they'd already filled my job with a girl Natasha's age. I'm so ashamed. To be such a fool."

"This is awful." Lera didn't know what else to say. If it weren't for the weakness of Lidochka's voice and her smudged makeup, it might have been a joke someone told at a party. "You need to go and ask for your money back," Lera added firmly.

"I did go back, and you can only guess what kinds of names they called me. There's no decency anymore, Lera." Her eyes were dry with conviction now. "No decency and no fair play."

She was glad to be alone in the metro again, in the splendor of its vaulted ceilings and mosaics, away from the sickly touch of misfortune. She took the red line to the Library of Lenin and transferred through its maze of halls and escalators to the

Arbat line, emerging out of the templelike station and crossing the Boulevard Ring until she was on the bright, populated strip of the Noviy Arbat. She was looking for the
Citibank office, to pick up more cash, since the window job
had cost more than she'd expected. The quick pace of pedestrians on the street carried her along. Being part of the purposeful, business-day life of the city was lifting her spirits.
You needed a certain kind of desperation, she thought, to
wander into the type of trap Lidochka had entered. It wasn't
enough simply to be foolish. It came from living too long inside a fantasyland of your own hopefulness. She felt grateful
for Grisha, whom she'd trusted to make sensible choices for
the both of them.

She found the glassed-in office of the Citibank on the
corner of the main plaza, across from a café whose oily shish
kebab smells now clogged her nose. It was a nice feeling to
open those heavy glass doors, slide your bank card into an
ATM machine, and watch the crisply ironed bills come out.
She stuck the bills in her purse and then, to restore her spirits a little more, touched the glass monitor to bring up her
and Grisha's current savings. She saw now that the various
accounts added up to less than $200,000, not even half of
what she remembered depositing after the house was sold. In
the past week alone, there had been three large transfers.

Grisha must have decided to keep some of their money at
a local bank, she thought, on her way home.

Inside the shuddering, speeding subway car, Lera made a
mental note to ask him later. She watched two adolescents
engaged in heavy kissing on the seat across from hers, pressing themselves up against the large circle of the Moscow
metro map. The girl looked like a rag doll, with her striped

stockings and limp bangs, and was gnawing on her dense-
looking boyfriend's lip. Every few moments her eyes flickered around the subway car with calculated satisfaction.
They'd probably met only a day before, these teenagers, but
already they knew it wasn't love unless it could be shown off
to the whole world. The lovers in this city made such an
elaborate production of their affections, especially consid-
ering that the natural expression of everyone else was either
dour or resentful. But then again, making elaborate pro-
ductions was a specialty here. Lera thought of Lidochka
again. To put an ad in the paper and interview a desperate,
hopeful woman for a job that didn't exist, in order to fill
some third-rate bus tour. They went to such lengths here to
fool you.

The kissing was still going on when the doors opened at
Lera's stop. At the turnstiles she glimpsed a young man with
a cardboard on his chest that read "Money for Prosthesis."
His sleeves were tucked in on themselves, flaccid flaps over
which he wore a long hunting vest.

It seemed that fraud was everywhere, once you paid attention. It was like the stray dogs you suddenly noticed all over
the city, trotting around the market, lying curled up beside
the heat vents in the metro underpasses. Fraud made up a
good deal of the local news coverage, she realized in her
kitchen that evening, watching the TV atop the refrigerator
as she ate the mushroom soup she'd reheated. On news, she
watched a woman being led away from a hospital in hand-
cuffs. The woman had checked herself into eight different
clinics with phantom illnesses and persuaded the other female patients in her wards to lend her money for a child (also
phantom) who was going hungry at home. For a con it cer-

tainly seemed like a full-time job, Lera thought. On the small screen the woman was raving that she hadn't stuck her hand in anyone's pocket.

Lera turned off the television, unable to watch anymore. They justified their deceit by convincing themselves that truth—if you took a close enough look at it—was no different from the lie, that even the principles of morality and lawfulness were themselves only lies by which the clever outsmarted the dumb. She walked into the bedroom and undressed. She missed Grisha; he hadn't called to tell her about his presentation, and his cell phone seemed to have been turned off. Outside the window an arrow-shaped sign pointing to a jeweler's shop flickered erratically. The snow had started falling, in tiny flakes at first and then in thicker chunks slanting down from a dark, milky sky. She crawled into bed and reached for the book on Grisha's nightstand. It was from a series on the lives of "The Great and the Famous," the sort of book he liked to read. When he'd quit Hewlett-Packard, he'd brought home books about moguls, biographies of CEOs, and read them in the basement, then repackaged his applied math background as a boon for Wall Street, where the winds had started blowing in the direction of quantitative analysis.

She opened to the introduction and thumbed through the first pages, about Pavel Ryabushinsky's ancestors, merchants descended from peasants of the Ryabushinsky community, Old Believers who'd launched a sackcloth business that survived Moscow's fire of 1812 and left them well positioned to buy up looms and weaving mills. Later the Ryabushinskys would import machinery from Manchester, send their sons to study abroad, enter the mortgage-banking business. All until the October Revolution, when Pavel Ryabushinsky and the rest of the clan fled to France. Lera turned the page. Like some of his western counterparts, Ryabushinsky considered charity his sacred responsibility, held progressive views, and wanted to improve the lot of his countrymen. Until his last days, living in France, he hoped to be useful and come back to his beloved Russia when the Revolution was toppled. But alas, he was not destined to return. This line was underscored faintly in pencil. Next to it was a note, handwritten into the margin: *He wasn't fated, my rabbit, but you are.* Lera looked at the message curiously. It was unmistakably a woman's hand. Its author had signed it simply *T*.

Lera touched the cavity of her neck. Her heart was galloping. She tried to steady her pulse with a deep breath, but the walls of her throat were closing up. T. Her mind was drawing a blank. *My rabbit*—sounded like the endearment of some sentimental tart. Had the book been a gift? A souvenir of a casual dalliance that might be over by now? Was it possible that Grisha had skipped that page and the inscription? Or had he left the book there to savor, certain that Lera would never open it? She remembered the words (had they been her mother's?) that on such occasions there were only two options: to leave or not to know. Nothing in between. Well, where was she to leave to? The house in Dobbs Ferry had been sold, the bank's check deposited, the furniture taken to consignment shops. And not to know—wasn't that always the intelligent option? It seemed that so much of marriage, hers at least, was made up of these negative spaces, the words she'd kept herself from saying, all in the service of not polluting daily conversations with unnecessary poison. And what good had it done her? She threw the bedcover off, her feet, her underarms clammy with sweat. She opened the window and breathed in the frost-laden air. The cold was like a remorseless living presence descending on her and gripping under her nightgown. She stared at the snow until she felt herself floating up, out of her numb skin.

It sickened Lera to have to call Olya in the morning. She could think of no one else who could tell her what was going on with Grisha.

"He hasn't called us in a month," Olya said. It was hard to tell if she really felt snubbed or was only feigning insult. "Must be a busy season for him."

"Let's not be so delicate. If he had someone else, you would tell me, I hope."

"You know me, Lera. I don't stand over anyone's business holding a candle." The hesitance in her voice suggested she didn't want to say more on the phone. "I need to drive to Mamontovka today," Olya said. "Why don't you come along?"

Olya steered her Acura with one hand resting atop the wheel. The gold tooth Lera remembered in the corner of her smile was gone. She'd cropped her hair, which played up her Tatar features, the wide cheeks and profile that looked as if it had been pounded flat by a small hammer. The Mamontovka Lera remembered had changed as well. Some of the wooden dachas had been rebuilt as year-round residences. A cottage town was what Olya called it now, though the "cottages" had nothing in common with the cozy, quaint ones of Westchester. These were more like fortresses you'd have to take by tank—three-story ski lodges rising from behind two-story fences.

"I think a woman lives alone in that one," Olya said. It was a Tudor but built with actual gables and turrets like a little medieval castle. "They shot off the husband last year."

"Shot *off*?" Lera said. "What is that, like too many elks, population control?"

Olya turned onto a residential street with fences on either side.

"It's tacky to put up a fence if you live on less than four acres of land," Lera said, more to the window than to Olya, and then felt a kind of shame at her own snobbery. She wasn't in Westchester anymore.

Olya drove down to where the road forked. An austere brick church stood in the middle of what might have been a small athletic field, the earth around it overturned by excavation. Olya parked the car and walked around to the side of the building. Boot prints and tracks had frozen in the hardened sludge. In the stillness and chill outside Lera could hear the guttural cawing of a crow. She craned her neck back to look at the vaulted roof that was helmeted by two blue cupolas. There was space for one more, which had not yet been erected. The sign on the brick wall read, "Church of the Icon of the Holy Mother of Unexpected Joy."

"They started restoring it two years ago," Olya said. "And by restore I mean tore it down and built it up again. You can imagine the cost."

Olya hunted for a napkin in her pocket to wipe her nose, damp like a puppy's from the cold. "When Grisha was visiting us in June, he said he wanted to meet some people who could help him. People with money. So we brought him here. First we introduced him to Father Alexander, who introduced him to that developer Mitin and his wife, the ballerina. Too old to stick her leg up in the air now, so she gives away her husband's money. Well, didn't they love Grisha! Blessing his soul, saying it was God who'd brought him back. We thought Grisha was playing along at first. You won't get far in business nowadays being an atheist. First everyone attended party meetings, now it's church."

The modest attack of sympathy on Olya's face couldn't disguise the pleasure of finally delivering this information. "But you have to show you're serious. You have to . . . make a gesture."

"And how much does a gesture cost these days?" Lera asked.

"Thirty thousand dollars won't get you canonized, but it'll get your name whispered."

"Ha!" Lera's laugh entered the air with a cloud of breath. "What other good news do you have for me?"

"I suspect he doesn't call us because he knows the talk has reached us. She works at a gallery, one of those avant-garde places that sells things you can find in a dumpster. She used to talk about *energetics* and UFOs. Now she crosses herself whenever a bus passes."

Olya walked up the steps of the church and tested the brass handle. The door was so small that to enter it one had to bend to a posture of humility. Lera tightened her coat and followed Olya inside. Two old women nodded kindly as they entered. The church smelled of candle wax and wet plaster, and most of the space had been sectioned off with scaffolds for construction, leaving just a high-ceilinged room the size of a small cellar. A makeshift altar and brass gate had been set up, with wooden icons to the left and right of it. Unlike everything else inside, the icons looked old, their wood battered and gouged. Lera approached one, an image of the Holy Mother, silent pain in her flat, painted eyes. The icon was

behind a protective sheet of Plexiglas, already covered with
waxy pink marks, left behind by some passionate believer who
hadn't bothered to wipe off her lipstick. Lera touched her
hand to the Virgin's and brought her fingers to her lips. Her
grandmother had taught her this: the proper way to kiss the
Lord and Holy Mother was on the hand, never on the face,
the way you'd kiss your drinking buddies. Lera closed her
eyes and tried to pray. Even here, under the domes into
which a good portion of their savings might have gone, she
wanted to ask God for justice. She prayed that Grisha would
remember himself.

On Saturday Grisha returned. She heard the squeal of the
hinge and smelled his damp jacket in the corridor. He walked
into the bathroom first, and locked the door. From the
kitchen she could hear him washing his hands and taking a
long, powerful piss, then washing his hands again.

"They know how to do everything here," he said, coming
in to where she sat in the kitchen. "Win gold medals, send
rockets into space. Only thing they don't know how to do is
wipe their own asses."

Lera stared out at the activity on Bolshaya Cherkizovskaya,
where the traffic never ended. She turned to look at him. His
hair was matted down on his high, bald forehead. He reeked
of smoke and sour sweat from the train. "Champions in
everything," he said, finding a bottle of cognac in one of the
cabinets. He poured three fingers of it into a narrow juice
glass and drained it in one gulp. Then he poured another.

"I offer them a *guaranteed* revenue. The problem is they
can't hide the profit. If they can't see a way to steal, they're

not interested. Try to show them how to *build* an industry from the bottom up, it's like explaining bronze to cavemen."

He finished off the second glass and sat down.

"It isn't an earthquake, Grisha," she said. "We can always go back. You had a good job. You can find something similar."

She tried not to think about how she looked right now, about the loose skin under her eyes from a night of no sleep. She hated herself for the way she was speaking to him, the voice of a lifetime of appeasement.

He squinted at her. "Have you been listening? Are you saying you want me to return to where some imbecile who's attended two management seminars can tell me, *You can do better?*"

"A lot of people would have wished for a start like yours, Grisha."

"*Start?*" He laughed. "Eleven years later, and that start was nothing but my finish line."

She got up and went to the windowsill, where she'd left his book. She opened it on the table and laid her finger on the margin. "After you told me to sell our *house*, told me to join you—I find this!"

He studied the inscription with a contorted, inscrutable expression on his face.

"Now I learn I don't know you. And what's more, I don't want to know you."

He flinched a little when the book hit his chest, then edged his chair back to pick it up off the floor.

"The house," he corrected, "was mine. I paid for it while you slept till noon."

He got up, the book tucked under his arm, and walked out. It took her a moment to understand what he was saying, as though her mind was awakening out of a spell. She gazed around wearily, her eyes alighting on the wilted plants on the windowsill. She followed after him into the corridor, where he was putting on his shoes.

"Where are you going? To this *bliad*?" The words didn't sound like they were coming out of her mouth, the shrillness in them seemed forced.

"Don't talk about what you don't know. Whatever obscene ideas you have are only in your own godless head. She's been celibate for two years," he said. "She's a *zatvornitsa*."

Now *here* was a word she hadn't heard in thirty years—a sexual hermit! And he didn't seem to care that she knew. He couldn't possibly be making this up. Celibacy! Well, these sluts had *really* gotten sophisticated.

Grisha plucked his jacket off the line of hooks by the door. She reached for his arm. "Whatever happened before I arrived, I've forgiven already." Her voice had gone needy, as soft as a rotting fruit. "We don't have to talk about it. Just stay."

His face was a soundless picture of loathing. "Let's not humiliate ourselves tonight," he said.

She placed herself between him and the door handle. "If you leave now, I promise you I will have the locks changed."

"This apartment doesn't belong to you," he said. He walked back to the bedroom. Lara followed him in.

"It's ours," she said, her voice breaking.

"I inherited it. I know the law." He found a squashed duffel bag at the bottom of the closet. In another few minutes, she sensed, she would be on her own. She felt it in the way she knew people felt their mortality, very suddenly, as knowledge deeper than shame or anticipation.

"Is it one of those midlife things?" she said. "You want to

grow your hair long? You want to buy a motorcycle? I'm not stopping you. But to give our money away like that, to a church!"

"You expect me to give it all to *you*? I'm done slaving away. You didn't even like to drive me to the station in the mornings. I had to run to catch the train and sit down sweating."

"Don't you dare throw that at me. I didn't make your meals or clean your house? Or raise your child?"

"I forgot, you bought a guest book for the bathroom. So everyone could sign their names when they shat, like they were at Buckingham Palace. You even hired someone to clean. The *chemicals* gave you headaches! I would have been here years ago," he said.

"If what?"

He didn't answer. He was dumping the folders and books on his desk into the duffel.

"Did you plan this?" She pictured herself making phone calls, tonight or tomorrow morning, to freeze their accounts. How much of their money was already gone? "Did you bring me here for a quick and cheap divorce? To cheat me out of everything?"

"What exactly, I'd like to know, would I cheat *you* out of? Explain to me where you got that stupid entitled idea? At the divorcee colony you call a gym?"

"And Masha?"

"I've always taken care of her. She'll understand me."

"You think I won't hire a lawyer?"

"Do what you wish," he said. "You're not among your *americaners*. Here they don't eviscerate a man for the crime of having a job."

"I don't know what that woman made you drink, Grisha." It was difficult to keep the tremor out of her voice.

He avoided brushing against her in the doorway as he carried the duffel.

"Where do you expect me to go?"

"You'll get along," he said.

When she returned to New York, her friends met her with arms open. They competed to help her, appropriately outraged by what Grisha had done. They praised her for having enough sense to freeze whatever money was left in the joint accounts. They were compassionate and practical and let her stay in their houses until she found an apartment. Drove her everywhere until she bought a car. But their eyes did not fool her. Their gratitude for the normalcy of their own marriages was almost like an awkward lust. At first they told her she shouldn't blame herself for what had happened. When she voiced her suffering in their living rooms, they listened closely to the parts of her story that confirmed that her common sense had gone slack. That she hadn't looked at her accounts for months, that she'd let Grisha go alone to a city where someone would steal your husband if you so much as got up for a minute to take a piss. After a while they seemed to have no reaction at all to her story, which was what made her stop telling it.

When she was working again, in a lab at a medical research park in Eastview, surrounded by test tubes and electrophoresis trays, she had a lot of time to think about Grisha. She imagined failures and disappointments for him in proportion to his smug, magnanimous "principles," in proportion to his pietistic love of his soil, his secret belief that he deserved to be a national hero. She imagined him bankrupt, drinking at eleven in the morning. She imagined him in a coffin surrounded by strangers and none of his old friends. But sometimes this hatred broke like a wave, unexplainably collapsing under its own weight, and before it would begin to well up again, she suddenly felt nothing but pure compassion for him, a kindness and forgiveness that almost broke her heart.

THERE WILL BE
NO FOURTH ROME

LARISA'S WAS AN OLD APARTMENT. Large, with high ceilings and wide, crisscrossing parquet boards. The parquet, like the chairs and table, had been bleached by light from the balcony, a narrow cement structure that opened to a wild yard two stories down. It was eleven in the morning, and I was on the balcony searching for the laundry I'd hung out the night before. I glanced down at the ferns and shrubs: between a patch of skinny birches a stray plastic bag was getting tugged and jerked in the wind. I had been staying with Larisa in Moscow for a week, and whenever I looked down into the yard I thought I was seeing the blurred outlines of footpaths, the turns of old gardens. It could have once been a tidy park, I thought, now abandoned to weeds. But then again it may always have looked like this, for all the fifty years the apartment had been in Larisa's family.

My mother had told me Larisa was old Moscow intelligentsia, though technically "old" went back only as far as two generations in a place like Russia, where the real old intelligentsia had fled or been shot during the Revolution. Larisa's father had in fact come from Belarusian peasant stock and had risen to become a diplomat in Hungary and China, and then had taught at the Institute of International Affairs, where Larisa herself had studied. But all these honors and distinctions meant nothing to Larisa, my mother had also said, for Larisa judged people by "the reflections cast off their soul," which in Mama's lexicon was just another way of saying that Larisa wasn't an anti-Semite.

I was still looking for my laundry when Larisa surfaced from her bedroom. She was wrapped in her old lavender bathrobe. Pieces of her steely blond hair stuck out at angles from her head. She looked at me, and then beyond me at the bright morning. "Did I sleep in again?" she said, rubbing an eye. "I got up at five this morning. Mur woke me."

The cat crawled out of the bedroom and leapt onto the plastic sheeting of the balcony's edge. He was black and, like all cats, a little obnoxious.

"Have you seen my clothes, Aunt Larisa?" I asked.

Her eyes were still foggy from sleep or myopia. "Oh yes." She raised a palm to her forehead. "I thought it might rain this morning. I took them down and hung them on the pipe." She turned around and shuffled back to her bedroom, slippers scratching the floor, and returned a minute later with a tidy folded stack.

I carried my clothes into the study, where I slept, while Larisa went into the kitchen for a cigarette. She'd made it a point not to smoke anywhere else in the apartment as long as I was there. Why she had decided to limit her tobacco to the place where we ate, I didn't ask. Like the bathroom, the kitchen was a room of mere function to her. Larisa made no rituals around meals and our dinners usually consisted of boiled hot dogs, cucumber salad, and tea. Occasionally she'd open the freezer and poke around in the permafrost until she found a stiff bag of *pelmeni*, then throw those in the boiling water, too. Still, every evening when I returned she made sure to ask if I was hungry and, whatever my answer, would start boiling water at once.

Larisa Lebedeva was an old friend of my parents'. Or rather she'd become their friend when she'd married my father's boyhood pal Alexei. When my parents and I had flown to Moscow sixteen years earlier to complete the paperwork we needed to leave the country forever, the Lebedevs had put us up. It was a favor not many of my parents' friends were willing to extend, not wanting to be linked with those absconding the homeland. Four years after we left the country, Alexei left Larisa. But it was Larisa my parents stayed in contact with, believing that in spite of their longer record with Alexei, she was the one who now needed their support. These are only the ordinary patterns of divorce, and I am sure my parents' estrangement from Alexei would have been temporary had he not died a year later. When Larisa called them in New York to tell them of Alyosha's death, they had grieved with her as if she were his widow.

From the week we'd stayed with her as her guest on Boystovskaya Street sixteen years earlier, I had remembered Larisa as a tall, soft-spoken blonde in rounded octagonal lenses that covered half her face. She was one of those women who are at once both large and delicate. And she was exactly this way now, age having thickened her a bit in the hips. Also, she had traded the tinted French frames for more modern squarish ones.

I got dressed and went into the kitchen for breakfast. Larisa had cut up some black bread and a cucumber and set out a glass bowl of cheese spread. The windows were dashed open, but the smoke stayed inside, drifting in a pillow above our heads.

Larisa pulled up at the thread of her tea bag. She didn't brew her tea. "When are you meeting your friend?" she asked.

"Two o'clock," I told her. "Nona and her boyfriend are picking me up on Tverskaya."

"The German?" she said.

I nodded. "She's pregnant." I did a little thing with my brows. I didn't know why I was announcing this, apart from feeling guilty for leaving Larisa alone another day.

"Is he going to marry her?"

"I guess so. Why not?"

Larisa blew on her tea. "Men," she said.

I'd had trouble reaching Nona all week. Larisa's telephone was an old rotary that had its line fused with a neighbor's. Whenever I picked up, there'd be a busy signal, occasionally overlaid with the faraway quikchatter of Russian. Other times Nona wasn't home. When she called back, I was out walking around the city and she was forced to leave messages with Larisa. Finally we had caught each other and agreed to meet. She was taking the train in from Ivanovo today.

Nona Gabunia had been my mother's best math student. The Gabunias were also our neighbors on the outskirts of Tbilisi, in a cement neighborhood that was forever under construction. We had heard almost nothing from their family during the Georgian Civil War until Nona called my mother from Krasnodar, where the Russian government had given land to refugees from the republics, and said that one way or another she had to leave.

My mother searched for exchange programs; one summer she found Nona a job as a counselor at an international camp in Vermont. Another year as a short-order cook in Cape Cod. But the problem was always the same: the American embassy kept turning her away. She was single and pretty and didn't have residency in one of the capital cities. Girls like Nona didn't come back; they became nannies and, if everything went as planned, married simple American boys from their night accounting classes. To that end, my mother had even involved her next-door neighbor Justin, a man whose wife had walked out one day, leaving him in full care of their three-year-old, a little boy whose abrupt and stifled movements shared no resemblance to the agile reflexes of other children on the street. My mother had waited a week after Justin's wife had left, then knocked on his door and gave him Nona's e-mail and a passport photo. For several months he and Nona wrote to each other. I know this only because the real correspondence went on between Justin and my mother, to whom Nona was forwarding all of his e-mails for a line-by-line translation. She had studied French, unfortunately, not English. By this time she was studying at medical school in Ivanovo, and my mother was peppering her letters with lines such as "I love children, especially sick ones." But one day, when the wife's car reappeared in Justin's driveway, our hopes for Nona were dashed once again.

Larisa stood up and poured what was left of her tea into the sink. "I'm going out today too, Regina," she smiled gaily. "By myself. I'm going to be a tourist!" She reached up to the top of the refrigerator and pawed around for her pack of cigarettes. "I'm going to the historical library to look up my father's books. They might have my uncle's, too. I've always wanted to do that." She grabbed the pack and maneuvered a match from a tiny box by the stove. "Do you think I should take the cane or the umbrella?"

Larisa asked this question whenever she left the apartment. She preferred the umbrella. But in the metro only a cane could proffer any hope that someone might stand up and offer her a seat. Except that to hear Larisa debate it, most of the time the cane didn't do any good either. If anything, it just gave them reason to stare you down like it was your fault you were alive. No regard for invalids at all. She had fractured her hip in a fall and, for an entire year, had not left her apartment. Her boyfriend, Misha, had nursed her to health. Now she was living off her small invalid's pension and some of the money Misha made from his job at an aviation plant.

"The umbrella," I said. I got up, rinsed my dish, and left it facedown on the cutting board Larisa used as a drying rack. She exhaled a band of smoke into the window screen.

"I'll see you this evening, Aunt Larisa," I said, and headed out.

"How's this different from your plans for her and Justin?" I had asked my mother when I'd come home to borrow a suitcase. I had told her about Nona's pregnancy, which I'd learned of only when I'd called Nona to say I was flying to Moscow.

"I don't know this other man," my mother said. "I know Justin. *He* is a good man."

"But if I was your daughter, would you send me off to live

with someone I barely knew? Who didn't speak my language, and who had a retarded kid on top of it?"

"What do you mean *if*?" she said. "And why is everything about you?" She examined my face. When she didn't understand something, she had a way of scanning it as if she was looking for acne. "They gave you vacation time so close to tax season?" she asked skeptically. "Did you do something bad?"

"No," I said, and hauled the suitcase to the side door.

She turned to the sink and poured herself a glass of water. She didn't believe me. A thatch of penny-colored hair glittered on her temple. My mother hadn't grown her first gray hair until she was forty-five, and even now she only used henna, refusing commercial dyes because of the unnamed health risks. "Some vacation," she murmured to herself. She didn't see why anyone would go to that country. "Those people will insult you and humiliate you," she liked to say. "And it will cost them nothing."

I had called in sick to work, expedited my visa, and found a plane ticket. Then I called again and in a shaky voice dropped the words "family" and "emergency," leaving enough room for interpretation so our secretary could only imagine the worst. I was sure when I came back, I'd find a condolence card in my box signed by the entire office. A small part of me hoped Conrad would try to call me at home. There is an axiom in accounting which states that if bad data is entered into a system, the outcome will also be invalid. Garbage In, Garbage Out. Such was the nature of our romance.

I'd noticed Conrad right away, the first month I started working at C&R. He's one of those men who is like a collie, large and enthusiastic at strange moments. At any given time, if you are to watch him, his face will be scrunched up like somebody has just pissed him off. So when he breaks, suddenly, into one of his grins, you can't help but think that this change of spirit has something to do with you. Maybe it was the hot-and-cold thing that gave him the impression of being someone who'd peaked a little too early in life. A former athlete, maybe a swimmer, because he had the frame of one, but who'd let his muscles go soft. Right away I suspected he looked better with his clothes on than off, and that he probably knew it, too. I wasn't very far off about that.

I was hired in January, when the hours were still reasonable and not like the hours in the spring, when accountants start looking like the walking dead. When all they can do is sit at conference tables until one in the morning sipping coffee and giggling at the financial statements and spreadsheets in front of them, like teenagers experimenting with nitrous oxide. I hadn't spoken to Conrad then. He worked in sales, persuading discount stores along the coast to buy C&R's bar code scanners and credit card readers. People were still eating their lunches at the cafeteria then, and one day I'd found myself facing the buffet, mesmerized with indecision, until Conrad walked up beside me and laid his elbow, very entertainingly, on my empty plate.

I doubt I was the first person he'd pulled that particular magic on. A week before, I'd heard one of the secretaries say, "He loooves to throw around sexual innuendos," and knew immediately who they were talking about. They gossiped about him with the disparaging affection women reserve for men they pretend not to be interested in.

"His mom cleans houses," said one of them. "He just bought her a condo."

"Sounds like a good son."

"A provider." And then they'd both laughed.

"Did you see what kind of car he drives?"

"It's big," said the one still laughing. "And it's got a really low seat."

"He luuves his car," said the other, drawing out the "uuh" so it rhymed with "duh."

A few weeks later Conrad drove me home in his low-seated car, keeping one warm hand on my knee. And at the end of the ride I made it easy and invited him up. From the beginning our efforts were more compulsive than passionate. He left before it was light, that time and the next. Only a month later, when his wife was away, attending a conference paid for by pharmaceutical companies, and his daughter was sleeping over at a friend's, did he spend the whole night.

Whenever I think about what happened, I get stuck on that old proverb—look not where you fell but where you slipped. One Sunday morning he turned on the TV while I got ready to shower. A baseball game was on a sports channel I never watched. Conrad doesn't watch much baseball, either; he's someone who likes the game only for the statistics. I stepped out of the bathroom and stood in the doorway, looking at the tiny men run, followed by the swift pans of invisible cameras that hovered in space like satellites. "I've never gone to a baseball game," I said a little coyly. He twisted his head to look at me but seemed unsurprised. This is one thing about not growing up in America; you are always discovering new gaps in your education: names of gemstones, rules in sports.

"Then you should go," he said.

"Not by myself. I'd want someone next to me explaining everything."

He pulled me down to the bed. "I can teach you right now."

But I didn't want that. I looked at him for another second, and finally he shrugged in response. A more formal invitation was not forthcoming. I went into the bathroom and
Conrad went back to watching TV.

"Why can't you take me?" I said when I walked back in.
"What's wrong with doing something other than"—I thrust a
hand at the bed—"this!"

He had another look—one you could see as either sleepy
or amorous, a smile that told me he was too exhausted to
deny the charges. He could manage somehow to be arrogant
even when he looked defeated. "That isn't how I meant it,
Regina. You know I'd love to take you out," he said. "You
don't want to know what kind of chokehold I'm in right now.
I've got two weeks to make my numbers for the quarter, and
I can't even close a deal with my biggest buyer. He's been
pulling my dick by a string all month."

I sat down on the edge of the bed. "How big of a sale do
you need?"

"Eight hundred thousand." Conrad pressed his thumb
and finger into the pits of his eyes, then pushed himself off
the mattress and out of bed. "Story of my life," he said.

A week passed before I saw Conrad again. He caught my
elbow by the women's room. He must have been lingering
there, in the alcove with the brass drinking fountain, waiting
until I walked by to draw me around.

"Guess what I got?" He waved a stack of invoices and purchase orders. "If these land on your desk this week, will you
okay them?"

I snatched a look at the purchase orders. "You got them to
sign!"

"I just waived their restocking fee."

"That was the deal you made? So they can ship back every-thing next month?"

"They're just helping me out, Regina."

I glanced down the hall to the senior accounting office.

Conrad put his hands, with the papers, on my shoulders. "Come on, don't jump ship on me now. If you make a fuss about this to those shylocks, no way it's going through."

If you are a clear-thinking person, this is when you cut your losses. But it is never so simple: with someone new, you have to lay the groundwork all over again. At least I do. It wasn't until the bonuses were handed out that Conrad finally took me on a proper date. We drove out the first Friday of March, the roads to Connecticut stained and cracking from the salt. He studied the menu of drinks while I watched the dimming and turning of the sky above the Mystic Seaport, through the inn's tall windows.

"Are you having a good time?" he said.

I nodded.

"You have to learn to relax, Regina. I can hear it."

I looked at him, his hair still wet from the shower he'd taken. Nice, lightly wavy hair that always looks best right be-fore the next cut.

"Your mind. It's always *ticking*," he said. He drew my hands together and bent down to kiss them, in gratitude.

"I need a ride to work," I asked one morning a few weeks later. I'd left my Impala in the shop, knowing he'd be spend-ing the night.

"I thought you wanted to be discreet about this."

"What?" I said. Where did he learn these bait-and-switches? "Co-workers give each other rides all the time."

"You're the one who's been ignoring *me*."

"Why would I do that?" I said.

"I thought you didn't want to act too cozy while they're looking into the deal."

I felt the roof of my mouth become dry.

"You were right," he said. "They returned all our merchandise."

"You said they weren't going to."

"I said they *might* not."

He'd turned around and started putting on his jacket. "Don't worry. People know that new accountants forget to flag return charges. It happens all the time."

"Are you dumping this on *me*?" I said.

"Calm down. Nothing's gonna happen to you. You haven't been working here very long. Just say you didn't know all the rules."

"You *asked* me to help you!"

"We made a mistake. It happens."

"That's real artful," I said, following him to the door. "I get nailed while you stand around like an ignorant Boy Scout."

He looked at me as though I were the ignorant one. "Fine. Drag me in and the SEC will call it fraud. It's up to you, Regina."

We drove along the Saw Mill River Parkway. I kept my window rolled down to feel the spring chill on my neck and ears. I glanced at his profile, which was the first and last thing I'd ever liked about Conrad. The handsome ridge of his uptight brow, the nostril that was like the quick hook of some crochet needle, and the million-dollar chin. The first time I had seen his profile, I'd thought: I could have sex with a profile like that.

He turned up the heat fans, in spite of my open window. I suppose he was still pretending I wasn't sitting in his car. He fiddled with the radio, scrolling from talk to music, which somehow made our silent situation all the more excruciating. We were on Route 9-A now, almost at our office complex, when Conrad slowed down and pulled over into the parking lot of the Saw Mill Multiplex Cinemas.

"You're making me walk?" I said.

"Jesus, Regina. We're less than a hundred yards from the office. It's a two-minute walk."

I stepped out and slammed the door. The car circled around and started to climb up the parking ramp. I'd been sweating and my skin was suddenly cold with moisture. I stood between the yellow parking stripes of the multiplex and watched Conrad's Camaro glide back into traffic. And then, in the early moments of despair, I became possessed with the sensational and radical idea of walking into the movie theater and spending the rest of my day nestled in its easy velvet darkness. I walked across the asphalt and up the wide steps of the cinema and pressed my forehead against the plate-glass doors. The place was empty. I turned back and saw there were only two cars in the parking lot. The others would not start arriving until one o'clock in the afternoon for the first matinee screenings. There was nothing left to do but walk the quarter-mile to work.

I slid my badge through the slot and entered the lobby. Before I climbed up to my world of desks and plastic dividers, I tried the doors of all the fire exits and found, behind one, a heap of cardboard boxes. From my desk I dialed a car and started packing. I left all my papers as they were and dropped into the box only my personals: three pairs of shoes that had accumulated under my desk, a few vials of dried perfume rolling around in my pen drawer, and a crushed Milky Way bar with its cold caramel scent. I carried the box out under my arm and took an elevator to the lobby, where I waited for the taxi to take me home.

On Friday I waited for Nona by an entrance to one of the underpasses on a crowded Pushkin Square. A boy of around sixteen was leaning unsteadily against the marble parapet, shaking the last drops of his beer into his mouth. His friends had tossed their bottles over the rampart and shouted for him to move it. He wobbled, then looked for a place to plant his bottle and decided on the spot right by his feet. "Young person!" a woman street-cleaner shouted down at him. "Young person!" He ignored her and lumbered unsteadily down the steps. "Retard," she called again, and returned to her sweeping.

From behind the parked cars I heard my name. "Regina!" a tall young woman was shouting. Her hair was dark, cropped closely around her face. In the passport photos Nona had sent us, she'd had a long, ash-blond braid.

"Your hair!" I laughed when she came close.

She threw her arms around me and gave me a narrow-eyed smile. She had heavy outer lids that made the inner lids all but invisible and gave her eyes a sad, ancient, sexy look.

"I can't color it while I've got this," she said, and patted her stomach.

"That's a myth."

"No, no!" she said in earnest horror. "All those chemicals. I would never do that to any child of mine."

Mentioning the baby, she turned to the man escorting her. "This is my future husband," she said with practiced friendly confidence.

"Dieter," said the man, leaning in to shake.

"Dieter is from Frankfurt," said Nona. He nodded, confirming. He looked about forty-six or forty-seven. His hair was a mix of several different grays and his cheeks sank in like the faces of men in coin portraits.

"Dieter has to go back to work," she said. "I thought I'd give you a tour of our warehouse." She led me to the car, then sidled in beside me in the back. At closer view her face was covered with hot, rosy blotches. "Have you thought about who's driving you to the airport Sunday?" she said, placing a custodial hand on my arm as Dieter started the car.

"I can take a taxi."

"That woman, the one you're staying with . . ."

"Larisa?" I said.

"When I called, I offered to have Dieter drive you. But she said her husband would do it."

"Misha?" I was confused. "He's not her husband," I said. "Or I don't think he is."

"She said he was," said Nona.

I'd never heard Larisa call Misha her husband, even though he stayed at her apartment five nights a week. By Friday evening, she'd told me, he was always gone, taking the train to Saltykovka where he was building a dacha for his son and daughter. He had divorced their mother ten years before, Larisa had told me, and even now felt guilty. The only person to whom Larisa still referred as her husband was Alexei, who had died nearly twelve years ago.

We drove alongside the river, which reflected the dull luster of the sky. I'd noticed that even without clouds, the sky was rarely transparent. During my first few days in Moscow the pollution had felt suffocating, but now it seemed to add a sawdust luminosity to the city.

Dieter pulled into a fenced-in, unpaved lot. A guard, idling at the gates, nodded us in. A row of white vans sat parked by the warehouse, which resembled a corrugated iron box. A second, bored-looking guard inside sat behind an old wooden writing table. Dieter led us past him down the corridor, where the doors opened into mint-colored rooms with desks and monitors. I watched his back and could see the specter of a delicate frame in spite of the dense torso. His shoulders were sloping and as triangular as a madonna's. Even in her flat shoes Nona was taller.

The mint-colored rooms were really only one room, I saw, with several doors. At a corner desk a young brunette sat talking on the telephone. She laid down the receiver as soon as Dieter walked in and searched her desk for papers, one eye set on Dieter in grim determination. But her co-worker got to him first, catching him in the doorway with her own questions. That girl was pretty, though her eyebrows looked like they'd been scalded off and then repainted with a ballpoint pen. Without greeting, Dieter took the paper from her hand, scanned it, and pointed to whatever figure was the source of her trouble. She sucked a breath through her teeth as if looking at a painful sore, then took the paper and marched back to her desk on her chunky heels. These girls were young, I thought, and better dressed than Nona. But Dieter hardly seemed aware of this. I wondered if the quality of his attention was different when Nona wasn't around, but I couldn't imagine him acting in any way that might be considered playful or provocative. He'd said two words to me in the car and had smiled just once: at a red light when he'd spontaneously lifted his camera off the front seat and tried to convince Nona to let him take a picture of her.

"Let's go," Nona said now, as more people lined up with questions for Dieter. She hooked her arm into mine and led me out through the hall and into a massive room at the end of the corridor, where rows and rows of metal shelves made a neat grid of alleys. "Here's what we're looking for," she said, grabbing a box of pantyhose. She gave me a quick head-to-toe, then found a larger size. "You'll like these." She tapped her nail on the box. "They fight cellulite." She tossed the stockings into her bag and craned her neck to inspect the other merchandise. There were neck pillows and creams and massaging brushes and other items of a dubious therapeutic value. Nona grabbed whatever her eyes fell on and tossed it into the bag, until we were at the end of the row, where two older, stern-looking women sat at their respective desks. I guessed they were inventory guards, hired to keep the younger employees from stealing. They bore down their gazes on us, on Nona, in a way I found unsettling. Nona pulled up on the unbuttoned ends of her blouse and, without looking at the women, tied them at her waist so that her bulging belly was on display. One of the guards rolled her eyes, as if she'd seen this act before. Fifteen years ago these women would have been the gatekeepers to everything. They might be working in libraries or in shops, or sitting in some darkened office wielding rubber stamps, in charge of making someone's life miserable. But Nona was the queen here now, and she knew it. She grabbed more pantyhose off the shelves and stuffed them into her bag with impunity. And when she got to the door, she turned and smiled at the dowagers like a ballerina at the end of her act.

"Does this stuff really work?" I asked, holding up a tube of cellulite cream, while we headed up the stairs.

"Let's hope," she said. "But you still won't look like *her.*" She pointed to the model on the pantyhose. "That's Sergei's bride. He's Dieter's partner. You can't open any business here without a Russian partner. And he's ripping Dieter off."

On the second floor I could tell that the warehouse had once been a massive factory, housing machinery that might have been used to make shells or ironing boards. The first door opened to a room where half a dozen girls sat behind sewing machines, stitching together plastic packages for the pantyhose. Their hair flapped in the indraft of a giant fan aiming air at their faces. They looked to be in their twenties, though a few looked younger.

"Nona, *vi longen noch!*" spoke a voice behind us. It was a man in heavy denim overalls and a foreman's cap. So Dieter had brought in his own people to manage the workers.

"Otto!" Nona said.

"Wie lange noch?"

"Eine Weile noch," she said in an exhausted voice. How long had she been studying German? I wondered.

I took a step inside the sewing room while they talked. On one of the walls, and just above the heads of the seamstresses, hung glossy pages ripped from porno magazines. Oiled and muscular men posing with women or alone, their privates smartly covered up by tamer photos of partial nudity. I dug through my bag and found my camera, scanned the room for an angle. Some of the girls had stopped their sewing and looked at me. I raised the aperture and saw that my move had ignited a chain of glances around the room. There was a quality to their looks that was more coordinated than the gazes of the dowagers downstairs. I had stumbled into a bee-hive. "May I?" I said, though when you are nervous is not the

time to ask for permission. Eyes darted from sewing table to
sewing table. I heard a snigger in the back. It had come from
a tiny blonde by the wall with the porno pictures. So that's
their leader, I thought.

"They don't pay us enough for that," she said, getting a
laugh from the others. I tried to hide my embarrassment by
drawing my camera to my side and squinting up at the ceiling, as if I were a real photographer looking for perfect ambient light. And then I was rescued by Nona at my side. "I'm
hungry," she said. "Let me show you our cafeteria."

I put the cap on my aperture and glanced back at little
Dolores Huerta, who was entertaining the others by pretending to click a camera.

The cafeteria was really just a kitchen with two fat women
working the stove. I sat down at a table while Nona brought
us a tray of soup bowls. "Eat well for the baby," a cook called
after her.

"So where are you going to have it?" I said.

"In Frankfurt, where else?"

I lifted a steaming spoon of soup to my mouth.

"It's good, right?" she said. "He really keeps them fed
here."

"Guess what one of your teenage seamstresses said to me
upstairs," I said.

Nona looked up with a cold face.

"I wanted to take a picture, and she told me, 'They don't
pay me enough for that.' "

"Which one of them said it?" She was suddenly giving me
a hard, serious stare.

"I don't know," I said. It hadn't been a pleasant experience, but I didn't want to get anyone in trouble.

"Was it the little one, with the short hair?"

"I can't remember."

"It doesn't matter. I know which one it was. The little bitch."

"I was sort of impressed," I said, trying to make light. "It's a very American way to answer, 'They don't pay me enough for that.' "

"Right," she said. "Workers of the world. Why don't we just make a sign for her and let her picket."

I got back to the apartment at eight. Misha was home. He and Larisa were sitting in the kitchen, eating a dinner of boiled pork and cucumber salad.

"Hoa . . . where . . . you?" he said in English when I walked in.

"What?" I said.

"How *where* you?"

"*Where were* you?" I said, trying to clarify.

Misha shook his head.

"How *where* you?" he repeated slowly. From the day he'd picked me up at the airport, he'd been testing his English on me. He'd mentioned winning some English-language award when he was in high school sometime in nineteen fifty-something, and I didn't have the heart to discourage him.

"You mean, *how are* you?" I said.

"*Da!*" Misha nodded, and slapped his hands together.

"I am good," I said, speaking as slowly as he'd spoken to me. "How *are* you?"

"I . . . yem . . . faine," Misha answered, and broke into a wide grin.

"Would you like some meat?" Larisa said, getting up for a plate.

No thanks, I told her.

Just one piece, she said.

I wasn't a great lover of boiled meat, I said.

"You liked it two days ago," she said. And indeed I had. But that was when I'd thought it was beef. I didn't keep kosher. But I believed that as long as I didn't eat anything high *treif* either, I would at least be staying a parallel course. When, toward the end of our first meal of boiled pork, with only a few morsels remaining, I had discovered what I was eating, I'd placed my fork aside and subtly tried to take the last piece I was chewing out with my napkin. And when Larisa had asked me whether I didn't eat pork, I answered all too cowardly that the piece was too salty for my taste.

"How was your day at the library?" I said, changing the topic.

"Brilliant." Larisa closed her eyes and inhaled as if she were savoring fresh air. "It turns out my uncle wrote a book, too. A manual on running an orphanage. I knew he ran an orphanage after the Second World War, but I didn't know he'd written it all down. And how was your day?" she asked.

I told her about my tour of Dieter's business.

"Ah, biznis," said Larisa. "I remember it used to be very exciting." I'd heard the story before, how when everyone had been rushing to open up businesses in Moscow, Larisa's brother and his wife had opened a chain of flower shops. The money had started flowing in, and soon Larisa left her press department job at the Pushkin Museum to work in one of the stores. But she didn't work there anymore. She'd fallen and broken her hip in the shop.

As if the memory had reinflamed some old pain, she shifted in her chair and rubbed her palm against her hip.

"Do you think you might go back someday?" I said. "I mean, once you can move around better."

Misha looked at Larisa.

She shook her head. "No," she said definitively. "I don't talk to them anymore."

"That's not true," said Misha. "You talked to your brother two weeks ago."

"That was about my father's papers," she said impatiently, and turned to me. "They blamed me for my injury. His wife had the nerve to tell me I'd let the business down by falling on a flat place."

"That makes no sense," I said. I was trying to sound sympathetic, but I had the feeling she was leaving something out.

Larisa shrugged. "That's what happened."

I got up. Spending my days getting around the city's immense distances had taken a toll. I was ready for bed, even though the sky would be light for another two or three hours.

"Aunt Larisa?" I said. "You wouldn't have anything to read here that would be in English?"

I had deliberately not brought along reading material, so that I would have to force myself to read in the language of my childhood. Every evening in bed I would pick up some book from the shelves in Larisa's study and try to read a page or two before I fell off to sleep. It was a grueling exercise. The written language was fraught with delicate phrasings and traps of syntax I could barely navigate. After a week and a half I had actually gotten worse, for I'd begun to struggle against my own stupidity.

I followed Larisa into the study. Right before she'd broken her hip, she'd "redecorated" the apartment, which meant she'd pretty much taken everything extra—all her books and her collection of ceramic cats—and squeezed them into the tiny alcove where I now slept. With the couch folded out and my suitcase on the floor, there was almost no room for us both to move around. I sat down on the sofabed and watched Larisa explore the shelves for English reading material. I realized how much I loved that room and how much it summarized Larisa, with its gauzy white curtain and its outdated calendars of Chagall and Picasso, and the picture postcards of Édith Piaf and Frida Kahlo stuck in the glass panels of the bookcases.

"Here we are," she said, pulling two small books out from behind some larger volumes. In her hands were the collected plays of Oscar Wilde, in hardcover, and a tattered paperback of Dr. Spock's *Baby and Child Care*.

"Oscar Wilde!" she said, looking as if she'd just rediscovered the book after twenty years.

"Can I see the other one?" I asked.

Curiously she looked at the Dr. Spock and handed it to me. When she closed the door behind her, I undressed and crawled under the sheets. I perused the extensive table of contents and opened to the first section of real interest: Discipline. I read: *A child needs to feel that her mother and father, however agreeable, have their own rights, know how to be firm, won't let her be unreasonable or rude. She likes them better this way*. There was no reason to punish your children, Dr. Spock said, if you guided them along with a firm hand from the very beginning and didn't let them wander into too much naughtiness. I read through a few more sections: Aggression, Duties, Jealousy, and Rivalry, which together added up to a cogent treatise on most of adult human behavior. Spock's advice on diarrhea, motor skills, and fresh air seemed all to be aiming at one point: you can't change another person's character, though you *can* change their behavior.

Like a magnetized needle my mind turned again to Conrad: had I mismanaged him, allowed him to behave worse and worse, until now, when punishment was the only option? Except punishing someone always meant hurting yourself even more. I wondered at what moment things had turned. They seemed to have been going wrong from the beginning: that second afternoon in my apartment when we lay in bed, sweating under the tangle of the down comforter, Conrad had sat up against my oak headboard. "Tell me something you don't like about me," he said. "It can be something small."

My right arm was pinned under him. I hauled myself up and gave him a stricken look.

"Fine," he said. "I'll start. The way you plant your lips down, then move the rest of your face from side to side when you kiss me, like you're kissing a toddler."

He lifted the back of his hand, pressed it to his lips, and imitated me. He was right. I didn't kiss like that all the time, but it was my signature move the moment the two of us were alone, my way of being tender. But I suppose there was a momminess, or an affected marital quality to it too, that annoyed him.

"Now it's your turn," he said.

I watched him, stunned. "I don't want you to change anything," I said, taking the high road.

"Of course you do."

"I don't want to play this game," I said, and swung my legs over the side of the bed.

He was instructing me, I thought now. I had gotten it

backward: I was the one being trained. There had been entire weeks in the office when we didn't say a word to each other, when it seemed like all of it had ended for good. But then on some late night when a group of us would be out for happy hour on account of a birthday, and the crowd would be petering out at last, he'd walk up behind me and rest his fingers on my shoulders ever so gently. And it would all start over again.

The window was open, letting in the air from the cool night yard. I could smell the tart whiff of Larisa's cigarette drifting in through the screen. She was smoking out on the balcony, getting in her last fix of calm before heading off to bed. The pain of my last encounter with Conrad didn't seem quite so raw from the long reach of a new hemisphere. I was only a mind now, egoless and open, ready to see life as it was.

Larisa rapped lightly on my door. "I'm awake," I said, and she peeked her head in. "I almost forgot to tell you, your mother called."

I waited until I heard her go into her bedroom to join Misha, then got up and brought the yellow rotary phone, with its long wire, into my room. The dial was jammed again, and I finally got it unstuck with a firm finger hook.

"Hi, my love," my mother said. "I thought you'd already gone to bed."

"Guess what I'm reading?" I said. "Dr. Spock!"

"Oh, I adored that Dr. Spock. I followed his every syllable when you were little."

"They sold his books here?"

"Of course. He was very fashionable. He was like . . . our first little window to the West. And then when we came to America, I remember someone told me he was running for

president. It was so strange to me. I was even a little embarrassed for him because I didn't understand why he'd run for
an office he couldn't win."

"That's what people do to advertise their cause," I said, a
little pedantically.

"I know *that*," she said. "Now I do. That's how much I
didn't know back then."

I laughed quietly. It felt nice to hear her voice.

"I called you because somebody left a message for you
from work."

My chest tightened. "A man?" I said.

"I think so."

"You can't remember who called?"

"I didn't listen closely, it was on your machine," she said.

"You played my machine?"

"I just pressed the button when I came to water your
plants. You had sixteen messages. Your box was full. I
thought there were a few from me and I could just erase them
to free up some space . . ."

"I can't believe this."

"I'm sorry," she said. "There were quite a few from a Dan
Sorgen."

Dale Sorgen. Dale was one of the older accountants, the
intractable salty dogs who could turn anyone into a schoolgirl
with a few sharp words.

"He said he wanted to ask you some questions about an
audit as soon as you got back."

I'd stopped listening. The words were gathering into one
heavy meaning, rocks in a lake. "Calm down," I could hear
Conrad saying. "You're solid." Except that now they were
probably being forced to restate the quarter earnings, or else

an investigation had been ordered by the SEC. A knot of tears was clogging my throat.

"Regina . . . ," my mother said.

I didn't make a sound.

"Tell me," she said. "Just tell me."

"Mama, I'm sorry," I said. I started crying. I told her what had happened. It seemed somehow easier to confess all these things knowing she was on the other side of the world.

"Oh, my darling," she said finally. "Your day will come. But right now be smart. You confess, and *then* what—the millennium begins?"

Neither of us said anything for a minute. We just breathed on the phone, counting the wasted seconds of our precious long-distance time.

"So he was married?"

"Yeah," I said.

"Con-rad?" She spoke his name with a careful sort of amusement. "Sounds Polish."

I slept in late. I was flying home in two days, and my body felt ready to revert to its old circadian rhythm. I took the phone back into the living room and tried to dial Nona at Dieter's apartment. The rotary jammed. I scrolled it back to its old position and dialed again. No tone. I hung up the receiver and picked it up again. This time I could hear the chatter of another conversation on a cross line, but no drone. I'd promised to call Nona by noon. We'd planned to meet again this afternoon; her sister Ecca was taking the train in from Ivanovo to see me before I left. I picked up the phone again and cranked the numbers. It was dead.

"Aunt Larisa," I called, knocking on her door. She came out, wearing her loose velour sweatpants and a blue promotional T-shirt my mother had included in her gifts.

"I think the phone is broken," I said. "I really need to call my friend."

Larisa walked over to the phone, where I'd put it on the coffee table, and sat down on the footrest beside it. She lifted the receiver, listened, shook it around, then listened again. She pressed her thumb on one of the plastic knobs of the dial and released it. "I *told* Misha to fix this," she said. Then she slammed the phone on the table and lifted the yellow receiver to her ear again. No luck. She unplugged the tangled wire out of the jack and plugged it in again, wedging it in hard. She shook the receiver like a bottle of vinegar, as if that might dislodge debris that had tumbled in and was stopping the tone from coming out.

"Why don't I go out and buy a new one?" I offered. I had no idea where I'd go around here to find a phone.

"He promised to fix it," she said. "*Everything.* I have to do everything here myself."

I stepped closer. "Maybe I can find a pay phone."

"There *are* no pay phones around here!" she snapped. I flinched and stepped back. But just as quickly, as if she'd shocked her own system with her outburst, she pressed her forehead to the phone and began to cry.

"Alyosha would have fixed it," she sobbed. Her face was hidden in her elbow.

I turned to look at the cat for its reaction. Mur was sitting on his hind paws and watching Larisa. Like me, he seemed to be awaiting a sign of reprieve. When the sound of Larisa's breathing steadied, the cat got on his fours and moseyed over to her footstool. Then he threw his front paws up on Larisa's knee and, digging his claws into her sweatpants, ripped two neat holes through the velour.

"Mur!" Larisa cried out in pain and disbelief. "Look what you did!" she yelled at the cat, but her eyes were all despair. And suddenly, spurred to action, she stood up and headed to the door. "I'll get you a phone," she said. I heard the door close behind her and then a slight creaking of the ceiling as she entered the apartment above us. I followed the sounds over my head and then the muffled, uneven shuffle of Larisa's slippers as she traveled back down the stairs.

"We'll be okay," she said as she walked in carrying the neighbors' black and white phone. Larisa was clutching it proudly as though it were a new top-of-the-line model. She ambled into the living room and plugged it in. When she picked up the receiver, a long clear tone rang out.

"Call your friend," she said. "We have twenty minutes."

"What happened?" Nona said. "I tried to call you."

"Larisa's telephone didn't work."

"She doesn't have a cell?"

"A cell?" I said. "No."

"The poor woman," Nona said, not at all ironically.

Dieter was at the warehouse, she said, and Ecca was coming sometime in the later afternoon and going straight to Dieter's apartment. She gave me the address. When I hung up, I saw that Larisa was sitting on the couch with a heavy photo album open on her lap, and another one resting beside her. I got up from the footstool and sat down next to her.

"Look at him," she said, running her finger along the cardboard triangles of a photo frame. "So handsome. He looks just like your Teddy Kennedy, when he was younger." She was right: I could see that Alexei shared a certain resemblance with the men of Hyannis Port. His face was a little doughy but still robust and a bit prankish.

She turned the page to a picture of her father. Larisa looked exactly like him. In the photo he was dressed in a uniform and wore the dignified, knowing expression of the civic-minded intellectual.

"I took care of him, right here," Larisa said, and lifted her face up to look around the room. "He lived with me four months after his stroke. And that's when I fell and fractured my hip. I had to stay at the hospital after my surgery, and that same week he died." She looked at the photo and shook her head. I thought she might be crying, but when she raised her head, her eyes were dry. "I took care of him in his last days, and he died in somebody else's arms. That's my fate," she said soberly. "Even my own Alyosha didn't die in my arms."

"In whose arms did he die?" I asked.

"She was the widow of one of his friends. He said he was in love with her, so what was I going to do? That's how it happens. After nineteen years . . . not that it hadn't happened in little ways before. He already had the cancer by then, but he didn't know it yet. A year later he died in her apartment."

I turned the cardboard page of the album and lifted away the acetate sheet. The two adjoining pages were pasted entirely with photographs of Larisa herself. There were pictures of a young, long-haired Larisa resting her chin in her palms and pouting at the camera. There were pictures of a bare-shouldered Larisa, coyly glancing upward, looking chaste even as she tried to look provocative; she had that brand of Slavic prettiness: broad-cheeked, benevolent, and rural.

"He loved to get me to pose for him. On Sundays he'd take out his camera, and we would stay home all afternoon just so he could take pictures of me." On the opposite page was a somewhat older Larisa from the eighties, wearing more eyeliner, her wispy hair cut short and feathered.

"We weren't like other couples. We were obsessed with each other. We were one of those couples who didn't need anybody else. That was the kind of love we had."

"But he left you," I said.

Larisa only shrugged. "He called me his *Turgenyevskaya jenshina*, his Turgenev woman. I guess that's what I am. In one lifetime I can love only one man. And my heart will always be given to him."

She was talking about a dead man, I thought. The Turgenev woman! I wanted to tell her that such women probably didn't even exist until Turgenev put them down on paper. But I knew that didn't matter to her: they were as real now to Larisa as Turgenev's lilacs and linden trees and fishponds. Single-mindedly devoted, they were women who, like Larisa herself, lived at a slower tempo than everybody else.

"And what about Misha?" I said instead.

"Well, it's hard to be alone. He's got his own children. I don't know why he can't let me into that part of his life. All I ever wanted was for us to do things *together*, like a family. You understand?"

I nodded. Larisa got up from the couch and walked over to open the balcony door, which the cat was scratching with its restless paw.

I could hear the front door unlocking.

"Hello, hello, who's home?" Misha sang loudly, entering the living room. He looked at me, and then at the black and white phone. "A new phone?" he said.

"No." Larisa turned around to stare at him. "We have to

give this one back to Valentina Ivanovna. You never fixed our phone, and Regina needed it today."

He looked at me, as if to confirm that this was true.

"I'll fix it when I get back," said Misha.

"Where are you going?" said Larisa, raising her brows.

"You know where I'm going. I told you I'll be back in time to drive her to the airport."

"I thought we were going to do something together this weekend."

"Why?" he said, looking at me again. "Regina is here."

"She has plans," Larisa said bitterly. "She has friends to see."

That was my cue to take off and leave them to work out their troubles by themselves. I closed the photo album and laid it softly on the couch. "I'll go get dressed now." I smiled at Larisa, then got up and went to my room.

I searched my suitcase for a clean shirt and listened to them on the other side of the door.

"They can't get along without you for one weekend?" Larisa was demanding.

"I have to finish the roof."

"Let me go with you. I can leave Regina a key."

"And what are you going to do there? I'll be laying shingles all weekend."

"You always have a reason," she said in protest. "You have it very comfortable here. Work is close, your shirts are ironed. And on weekends I'm all alone."

"Is that what you think? I'm with you because it's convenient?"

"I don't know."

"You think I *want* something from you?" I could hear the

resonating tenor of Misha's voice through the door. "Because if that's what you think, we can end this right now."

And then it quieted down. I couldn't hear anything. Larisa was talking softly, trying to calm him. Or maybe they'd just become aware that they were within my range of hearing.

I pulled my hair up in a ponytail and spread a line of copper gloss on my lips. Then I gently turned the knob and walked out into the hall.

They'd stopped talking. "I'll probably come back late," I said. They stood in the middle of the room facing each other. Solemnly, both of them nodded, and I let myself out, closing the door behind me.

In the metro I was met by the usual ocean of dour faces. My God, I thought, these people have chandeliers in their subway. They have sculpted arches and mosaics. Their stations look better than the halls of some universities! Couldn't they at least be delighted about *that*? It was as if everyone in Moscow was suffering from exactly the same toothache. And soon enough I'd be suffering from it, too.

There was a tall gate around Dieter's apartment complex. The entire compound belonged to the German government and sat in an old section of Moscow. The streets were narrower; the high-rises had been replaced by rental houses of pale brick and pastel yellow. Even the sky seemed gentler here, a watercolor blue that turned coppery to the east.

Nona let me up. She unlocked the door and apologized for the clutter; she'd been moving her things in. The apartment was smaller than I'd expected—just one room and a fold-out cot right in the kitchen. It was a single man's apartment, and I wondered how Nona would find room for herself in it. There was a drafting desk in the corner, supporting a computer and fax machine, and next to that was a framed photograph of two boys, about ten and twelve.

"Those are his sons," said Nona, seeing me look at them. "That's Florian, and that's Thomas."

"He's divorced?"

"He's getting divorced." She dropped herself down on the couch. "I've got some more gifts for you," she said.

"You gave me enough yesterday."

She leaned over the side of the couch. "Those were from the company. These are from me personally." She lifted a small glossy bag and set it on the glass coffee table.

I kneeled on the carpet and took out the items one by one. There was a basket with fancy soaps, a cat's eye bracelet, and a bottle of apricot-colored perfume capped with a black tassel.

"This looks expensive," I said.

"I get it cheaper because I sell it."

I drew the perfume bottle close to my face and looked at the brand on the bottle. In tiny capitals the embossed glass letters read, AVON.

"You're an Avon Lady?" I said.

"I'm taking a break. I have a group of girls from the medical school selling now. You ought to try it. I made more on this than I did working in the clinic."

"I don't know." I smiled. I looked at her face and realized she was serious. I went back to studying my gifts. My conception of the Avon Lady was perhaps outmoded and a little kitschy. But I couldn't help imagining the pastel-colored woman of Edward Scissorhands getting rejected at every door until she finds herself knocking on the Gothic mansion on the hill.

"I don't think I have the time," I said.

"It's only a lot of work at first. Now I just sit back and collect commissions."

"I think it works differently in America." I put the perfume bottle on the table.

"Really?" Nona propped her hand on the armrest and, using her elbow for leverage, pushed herself up. "I thought it was the same model everywhere." She got up from the couch and made a limping circle behind me, heading into the kitchen.

It was seven o'clock but still light. I got up and followed her.

"Where's Ecca?" Nona said irritably. "Are you hungry? If she doesn't show up in the next five minutes, I'll have to start making something. I can't live in hunger."

She put a skillet on the stove and poured in some oil.

"So Dieter is getting divorced?" I said, taking a seat.

"They already know about me. Now it's just a matter of time." She moved the oil around on the pan. "He and his wife haven't slept in the same bed in six years." I thought about Conrad and how he liked to tell me that he and his wife hadn't slept together in over a year. As if it made a bit of difference to me. I found it amusing that men who cheated on their wives were so insistent on saying they no longer slept with them. Maybe it was some kind of a last tribute to monogamy.

"How did you meet?" I said.

"The Internet. How else."

"Were there others?"

"There was a man in Turkey," Nona said. "Never married. I went to Istanbul for two weeks to see him. With him it was love. But he kept accusing me. He thought I had someone here. My philosophy is: he whose own ass is dirty always suspects others."

"Love, huh?" I said. "And what about Dieter?"

"You know what my mother used to say about queens?"

"Queens?"

"Yes. A queen is not one who loves but the one who is loved."

Nona opened the freezer and took out a piece of fish wrapped in plastic, then stuck her hand in a paper bag of flour and poured a fistful on the cutting board.

"What about you?" she asked, smiling. While she cut up the fish and rolled it in flour and laid it on the skillet, I told her about Conrad and the circumstances behind my "taking leave."

"Ugh!" she said when I was finished. "Don't you just wish you could kill people like that with your thoughts?" She seemed to draw no parallel between my story and her own with Dieter. We ate, and while I was washing the dishes, Ecca arrived, in a flurry of laughter and kisses and apologies. The three of us set out into town.

Ecca hadn't changed much. She'd been a teenager when we'd left, and now she only looked more like herself, with deeper laugh lines. Next to Nona, Ecca was as skinny as a dancer. She looked like her father, with a cleft in her chin and a gap between her front teeth, but her eyes were bright and excitable, making her whole face incandescent with charisma.

Ecca said she was sorry she couldn't stay overnight to see me off. Mashka, her six-year-old, was sick again because the kid kept sitting down on cold surfaces. "I told her if she keeps it up, she'll freeze her ovaries."

"We never got sick as kids," said Nona. "That's what was great about Georgia. All that citrus."

We hailed a cab. Ecca sat down in the front seat while Nona and I took the back. We were driving along the city's Garden Ring, and I still couldn't find my seatbelt. There wasn't even a trace of one; it seemed to have been ripped out at the root. "Don't bother," said Nona, watching me struggle. I looked at the driver. He wasn't wearing his, either.

Ecca pulled her seatbelt to her left hip and held it down with her hand.

"Just leave it, Ecca," said Nona.

"No. What if a police car drives by?"

"Ecca, this is ridiculous. If you're going to hold the belt like that, why don't you just buckle it up like a normal person?"

"Because I don't want to." She touched her chin to her chest and looked down at the seatbelt self-consciously. "It isn't comfortable that way."

"It's more comfortable to keep your arm twisted?"

"Listen to you, bossy lady," she said, facing us.

"That's what I'm talking about," Nona said, turning to me. "Everything we do here is backward. We'll break the law, even when it's a million times easier just to follow it."

Ecca looked down at her seatbelt again. "Maybe it wrinkles my shirt," she said, not giving up.

On the radio a woman was talking about the eight hundred sixtieth anniversary of the city and the various renovations of its old churches. As the motto went, "The second was Constantinople, and Moscow is the third and final Rome. There will be no fourth."

"Where are you from?" the cab driver said, lifting his eyes to look at me through the long rearview mirror.

"Me?" I said.

"Listen to that," said Nona, aiming her chin at the radio. "What a dumb motto. 'And there will be no fourth.' Like this city is so worried someone might go off and build themselves a fourth Rome."

"Yes, you," said the driver. "You have . . . um, an accent."

"Take a guess?" Ecca said.

"It's a little hard to tell. Definitely not the West. Somewhere in the Baltic. Estonia?"

"That's right," I said. "I'm from Estonia."

Nona and Ecca exchanged looks. They were trying not to laugh.

"So how long you here?" said the driver.

"I'm leaving tomorrow," I answered. "Back to Estonia."

We rode a few blocks more. "You pretty women have a terrific night!" he said, before he dropped us off.

We walked down one of the side streets that separated Noviy Arbat from Old Arbat. The restaurant we were going to was called Déjà Vu, though it didn't serve French food. We were going there to hear a singer Nona liked, an Armenian diva recently dumped from a famous rock group. A red brick staircase led up to a restaurant with a carved-out two-level ceiling, fashionably painted robin's-egg blue. The band was tuning on stage, and the singer was welcoming everybody. She was dark haired and heavy and wore fist-sized turquoise jewelry on her neck and fingers.

I turned to Nona. "What does she sing?"

"Jazz," she whispered.

I watched the singer blow a kiss at the guests sitting right in front of her. Jazz, it turned out, actually meant R&B covers of Beatles songs. I sliced my small steak and listened to music in a language that sounded vaguely like English.

"They slipper why they pass, they slipper why across the universe . . . ," sang the corpulent siren.

Nona had her eyes closed and was singing along with a few key words. I watched the pools of sorrow and waves of joy drifting through her open mind.

"Nothing going to change my wood . . ." crooned the singer.

I took a few sips of water, and in less than a moment the waitress was at my side, refilling my glass. The waitresses in this restaurant didn't smile and didn't bear any of the ambient friendliness I associated with waitstaff, but they were doing their job.

Nona's eyes were still closed. Now the woman was singing about the many times she'd been alone and the many times she'd cried. But still they all led her back to the same "lawn and windy roar."

Nona's cell phone began buzzing in her bag, and her eyes snapped open.

"*Da?*" she said quietly. "*Da*. Hi, love." She stood up from the table and headed in the direction of the restrooms.

"Do you mind if I smoke?" said Ecca. "I'll put it out when she comes back."

Now that Nona was gone, I wanted to figure out the pregnancy question. "Listen, Ecca," I said, "I'm trying to understand the math here. She's been seeing him for how long?"

"Six months."

"And she's six months pregnant?"

"Exactly. I struggle for two years, and she gets pregnant

just by thinking about it. You know, I didn't even agree to marry Sasha until I became pregnant. I wanted to make sure we would be able to."

"But wait . . ."

"Yes, it's his. She got herself pregnant the week they met. I mean, they'd been e-mailing."

"But she didn't even know him," I said.

"She knew enough. Even if he does have all that gray hair and another family, he's still better than our losers."

"You don't mind that she'll move to Frankfurt?"

"I have a feeling that won't happen for a while," said Ecca. "Why would he go back now? All the money's here."

"She said, for the baby . . ."

"I'm sure he's telling her that." Ecca simulated a smile. "But listen, why do you think he's with her instead of one of those tarts from his office? Nona's got a motor in her ass. As soon as she moves all her stuff into his apartment, he's going to hire her to work for him. Did she tell you that? He knows he's getting ripped off by his partner. Dieter isn't stupid. He wants his own person around, to look after his business while he's back in Frankfurt with his wife and teenagers, building a second-story addition to their house, or whatever it is he goes back there to do."

Ecca shot a glance toward Nona, who'd snapped shut her cell phone and with a determined, sour look was heading back to our table.

"Hi," she said, planting herself down in the wicker chair. "Dieter says he'll be late. He'll try to come, but he probably won't get here before eleven."

Ecca put her cigarette out on the wet napkin. "It's fine, Nona," she said. "Forget about it. We're having a good time, aren't we?"

Nona closed her eyelids, breathed, then opened them again.

"What were you talking about?" she said.

"Our fertility," said Ecca, and crumpled the napkin. "I was about to tell Regina about my adventures with tetracycline. My first gynecologist was this old woman, seventy years old," she said, turning to me. "I got sick, and when I went to her, she told me I had a swollen fallopian tube, which was why I couldn't get pregnant. So she put me on tetracycline. I was working two jobs, then I quit one and finally got some rest. Boom. Two months, and I was pregnant with Mashka. So I went back to this witch-lady to tell her, and she suddenly remembered that she'd put me on the tetracycline and told me I wasn't supposed to try to get pregnant while I was on it. And I was probably carrying around a mutant now, so I'd better hurry up and get myself an abortion. For a whole week I cried, but I took my chances. And when Mashka was born, everything was in the right place. Five toes, five fingers."

"Our medicine is in the dark ages," Nona commented. "I practically have to bribe the nurses to sterilize my equipment."

"It's not *that* bad," said Ecca.

"The only thing we've ever known how to do here," Nona continued, ignoring her, "is measure each other's blood pressure. Remember that, when our parents threw those parties, after dessert somebody would always pull out the old pump-and-armband."

"And everybody took turns strapping it on," laughed Ecca.

I did remember. It had been like a sexy parlor game our parents had played, an excuse to have an intimate moment with somebody else's spouse.

Ecca laughed again and then returned to her own story. "When Sasha and I were still trying to have a baby," she said wistfully, "he'd always ask me, 'Katya, will you still marry me even if you can't get pregnant right now?'" She glanced up at the light blue ceiling and sighed.

Nona rolled her eyes, as if to say *how romantic*.

"Katya?" I said. "Your husband calls you Katya?"

"Katya, short for Ekaterina," said Ecca, shrugging it off.

"Nobody knows her as Ecca anymore," Nona said, smiling. "Only I still call you that."

"It's the same thing."

"No, it isn't," said Nona.

The table behind us was making a lot of noise, laughing at their own jokes. We turned around to look. There were several men, a few with longish hair and monochromatic silk ties. The women, who seemed even more gregarious, were wearing heavy French makeup and had the kind of classic Eastern European faces that straddled the line between trash and exquisite beauty.

"Look at them," said Nona. "Drown me if I ever start to dress like a new Russian."

"Isn't that what you are?" I said. "You're rich."

"I'm not Russian."

"You are," said Ecca, offended. "We're half."

"Well, I'm not changing my name," said Nona.

"I *didn't* change my name. And if you're such a big patriot, why don't you move back to Georgia?"

"I don't need to move back there," Nona said, looking straight at her. "I'm moving to Frankfurt." They seemed to have forgotten I was there, but I didn't stop them. In their sisterly way they were probably enjoying their bickering.

"We'll see," said Ecca, turning back toward the singer.

Nona's cell phone rang again, and once more she got up and headed for the restrooms.

"She's just being pregnant," said Ecca. "She loves to start these fights. I just go along with it because a good fight can be very fortifying. But sometimes I'm ready to kill her."

Dieter didn't join us that night. Nona and I rode with Ecca to the station and put her on the night train. It had started to rain, and in the damp street the gypsy-cab drivers beckoned us, but Nona, stepping off the sidewalk to inspect each one, in the end refused all of them for shortcomings she didn't give a reason for. We ended up taking the metro, and in the dry roaring silence of the car, we sat side by side staring at the blackened windows.

We were tired, or rather Nona was tired. My head was glowing from the glass of white wine at the restaurant. It looked like Nona was still upset about Dieter not showing up, but she didn't say anything about it.

"So you'll be packing tonight?" she said.

My plane didn't leave until six the next evening, I told her. I needed to be at the airport by three. Tonight I would just crawl into bed and read my Dr. Spock. "It's funny," I said. "I found an old copy in Larisa's apartment, in English."

"Does she have children?" Nona asked.

"No. But it turns out my mother read him."

"Hmm," Nona said. "Your mom was a real book mom. Ours was a folk mom. She was of that school of parenting that taught you to smack your kid's head once in a while with the side of a shoe."

We laughed and got quiet again. Perhaps it was the wine, or the nearly empty train car, but I felt scared for her all of a sudden. Her short hair was wet from the rain and stuck to her forehead as if she were a wet cat. Her lips were purple. She looked like she hadn't slept in a long time.

"Are you sure you want to go through with this?" I said.

"I think it's a little too late for that," she said, turning to me. And I realized I had been fixing my eyes on her stomach.

"That isn't what I'm talking about," I said. "Ecca told me you're going to work for him. Doing what: answering the phone?"

"Tell me what clinic is going to hire me in this city when they know I'll work for three months, then take off for maternity leave?"

"Maternity leave doesn't last forever," I said. "You've been training to be a doctor for six years."

"So what?"

"So you're just going to give that up?"

"I'd rather work for Dieter, and then we'll be living in Frankfurt."

"And what if it doesn't work out between you?" I said. "Then what? What if his business fails? Medicine changes, you'll lose your skills."

"Fails?" She looked at me like I was crazy. "We'll be selling stockings in every kiosk in this metro! And if that fails, we'll start another one."

"Or he'll go home!" I said. "You aren't even married."

Nona shook her head in disbelief.

"You. You are just so sure it won't work out."

"You don't know each other very well," I said calmly. "If I'm not wrong, he has another family."

She stared at me in amazement. "Do you have any idea what you're talking about? You've had one ridiculous affair, and you think you're the voice of experience?"

I didn't feel like talking about this anymore. I looked at

the woman sitting on the bench across from us. She was about forty, wearing the same upward-pointing shoes all the young people wore. They're all a big herd, I thought. Young and old. I was tired of looking at their grim, unfriendly faces. What was wrong with these people, with this whole city, where an ordinary smile was considered a sign of weakness?

"He won't leave me out on the street," Nona said flatly when we arrived at my station. We didn't kiss or hug. I walked off the train, and she stayed.

When I came home, Larisa was still up. I could see the light on in the kitchen through the wavy glass door. It was one o'clock in the morning.

"Long night," I said, walking in. Larisa was sitting at the table smoking a cigarette, with a plate of cottage cheese and a porcelain sugar bowl in front of her.

"Is Misha here?"

She shook her head. "He's at Saltykovka, with his family."

"You didn't have to stay up for me."

"It's okay. I couldn't sleep. How are your friends?"

"They're good. We talked," I said, pulling one arm out of the sleeve of my jacket, "about our fertility."

Larisa twisted her lips into a half smile and raised her eyebrows, which were almost invisible without the brown pencil lines.

"If you get more than two women in one room," I said, "the talk invariably turns to fertility."

"Are you done reading Dr. Spock?" she said, tapping out her cigarette.

"I don't think I'll read him tonight. Too much reassuring common sense for me."

"I saw you underlined some of it."

"I did? I mean, you looked inside?"

"I was just cleaning up. I was going to put all the books away," she said, then paused. "Unless you want to take it back with you?"

"Aunt Larisa," I said. "Do you mind if I ask, why do you have it? Why in *English*?"

She looked past me at the refrigerator. She seemed to be thinking about it. "I wanted to improve my English when I was twenty-eight. I thought I could practice reading it and at the same time . . ." She stopped.

"You were planning to have a child?" I said.

She nodded. "It turned out I had cysts in one of my ovaries, though. I'd had these pains for a while, but they never got diagnosed. One night I was in so much pain, Alyosha took me to the hospital. It turned out a cyst had gotten infected. So that night they did surgery to remove it, along with the ovary. And while I was under anesthesia, they cut out the other ovary too, as a preventive measure, they later said. In the morning the head of the ward came to see me. He hadn't been on call when they'd operated on me. He looked at my chart and said, 'Young woman, have you already had a child?' And then he gave me the news. That's our country," she said. "Slice it off now, ask questions later."

I gazed at her in disbelief, and she stared back without expression.

"I'm so sorry," I said.

"It's different when you have children. Who knows how things would have turned out between Alyosha and me if we'd had a child? Two people can't live their entire lives just being obsessed with each other." She folded her arms on the table.

"Or even now," she said. "If I had someone now, instead of just Misha."

I got out of my chair and walked over to her. While I held her, she pressed her head into the small of my shoulder. Her neck was soft the way skin gets when it becomes a little loose. I could smell her sweetness through the tobacco, and the last notes of the soapy perfume she kept on the sink. How many ways a person can be lonely, I thought.

I couldn't sleep that night. I kept closing my eyes to ease the headache between them and jerking awake again. Sleep! I demanded. Then I calmed myself by saying I would sleep on the plane. But the prospect of spending eleven hours elevated in the air, feeding on pudding, made me sick. My window was open and I concentrated on the fans of sound passing: distant voices being carried in the outdoor night, the long whooshes of cars brushing blacktop. Everything, divided by silences. I felt the hard cushions of the couch under my back, a seam where the sofa unfolded digging into the knobs of my spine. I was the Princess on the Pea. Nothing felt comfortable. I pulled the pillow from under my neck and stuffed it between my knees. Why had I opened my mouth? Here I'd come, from the wise end of the planet to offer Nona my Important Opinion.

I lay on my back. The walls were draped in gray. The bookshelves and desk were opaque shapes between murky rectangles of half-light. My mind, manic with thought, was now a warped door that wouldn't close. You can't demand so much of people and yet expect so little of them, it kept telling me. For the first time I contemplated the lace designs on

Larisa's transparent curtains: there was a border of round flowers, and butterflies swimming above them. The fabric creases were projected onto the ceiling. Sweet Larisa, who lived in the world of her love. It didn't matter to her that her husband had left her. Or that he was dead now. She had loved him and she was still proud of that love. I remembered all the times in my life I had begun to fall in love, *had* fallen in love, and then told myself I had been wrong. Because people, when you got down to it, always ended up being so disappointing. Sooner or later you discovered something about them that would make you ashamed of what you had felt for them. Or they made things simple by not loving you back. Love unreturned wasn't really love; it was obsession, vulgar and misguided. Except that for Larisa, the reality of what had happened to her hadn't thrown all her old feelings into question. It had not caused her to disown them. Foolish, naïve, embarrassing, they were hers and she would die with them. Really, it was a kind of freedom, I thought.

I heard a faint scratching at the bottom of my door. It was Mur, who must have gotten locked out of Larisa's room. In the dark I got up and turned the handle. The door pushed a crack and I caught his small black shadow dip into the room and disappear. I crawled back under the covers and, after a little pull-and-tug, felt a lump of fur-covered fat arranging itself on the top of my cold feet. I thought of a hen squatting on its nest. I pulled my toes out from under him and the lump squeezed itself beneath the arches of my feet. And then I fell asleep.

I woke up with the sun shining spots on the curtains. It was noon. Misha was arriving at two to take me to the airport.

"Your friend has been calling all morning," Larisa said as

soon as I stepped into the hallway. "I didn't want to wake you up. You looked so peaceful. Anyway, I already talked to her. She feels terrible about last night. Did you two have a fight?"

I opened my mouth, but Larisa didn't wait for me to answer. "She wanted to see you before you left, so I invited her here for tea."

"When?" I asked, my mouth still cottony.

"She called half an hour ago." There was a rag in Larisa's hand. She was tidying up the apartment.

"Go! Quickly," she ordered. "Take a shower. Pack your things."

I watched her turn and shoo Mur into her room. Cats and pregnant women didn't mix. "I'm sorry, Mur, we are having an important guest," she lectured. "You'll have to be alone for a while." And then she locked him in the bedroom.

I was getting out of the shower when I heard the door unlatch. I toweled off, dressed, and went into the living room.

"I'm sorry," Nona said, standing up from the couch. "I'm sorry for how I was behaving last night. I didn't want you to leave and . . ."

She was wearing a long dress and had her short hair up in a headband.

"No, don't be," I said, embarrassed. "I should be." She came up to me and we stood there, trying to smile with our lips turned down.

"Are you packed?" said Larisa, walking in.

I shook my head.

"Go, fast. Misha is coming soon!"

I kept my door open so I could hear them talking. Larisa led Nona into the kitchen. "How many months do you have left?" she asked.

Three, Nona told her.

She told Nona she looked wonderful, not even a little dark spot on her complexion. Did she know the gender?

"A boy," said Nona, feigning disappointment. "What can you do?"

"A boy! But that's wonderful," said Larisa. "A boy is a mother's defender!" She was playing her part, the cheerful supporter, and if Nona had told her she was carrying a girl, Larisa would have said, "How lovely! A girl is a mother's companion!"

"Have you thought about names?" Larisa was indulging her with all the questions pregnant women loved to get asked. Had she felt the baby kicking already? Was she planning to nurse? Nona was answering them all with delight. And so it went, that age-old duet of women. How had I not thought to ask these questions? I wondered. I had looked at her body and had seen nothing but another weight she was carrying. But having this baby wasn't something Nona was forcing herself to do out of necessity or circumstances. She was thirty-one and she wanted a child.

My suitcase was now heavy with all the stuff Nona had given me, creams and socks and massagers. I hoisted it on its side and dragged it out into the hallway.

"When you're all done moving," Larisa was saying, "if you need anything at all, you call here."

I entered the kitchen, drawn by an odor other than cigarettes. Larisa was actually brewing tea. She had placed the porcelain teapot in the middle of the table on a small wooden cutting board and covered it with a dish towel to keep the heat from escaping while the tea steeped.

"Sit down," she said, looking at me. "Stop moving around. Before a journey you always have to sit in silence."

She'd pulled out her *podstokaniki*, the silver-plated filigree glass holders, beautiful things engraved with trelliswork. When she poured in the tea, the clear glass steamed up but the metal handles stayed cool. "Okay," she said. "Now we'll sit." And that's what we did, we sat, waiting for Misha to arrive and for our drinks to cool, so we could inhale them in the warm afternoon.

ACKNOWLEDGMENTS

FOR THEIR TIME AND UNSHAKABLE FAITH I would like to thank
Aoife Naughton, Nadya Strizhevskaya, and Tatiana Krasikov.
For help in publication, Cindy Spiegel and Richard Abate.
My thanks to the first readers of some of these stories—
Roderic Crooks, Jen Bills, Lisa Srisuro, Sarah Strickley,
Anna Solomon, and James Renfro. Also to Alana Newhouse,
Connie Brothers, and Carol Christian for their encourage-
ment and kindness.